**"You're hiding something, Avery..."**

"And, yet, you had no problem putting your mouth all over me last night."

She felt Knox's reaction to her words.

"I can separate business and pleasure. My question, Avery, is can you?"

Twisting out of his grasp, she scooted off the bed and turned to face him. He could read the hunger there.

"Yes," she finally said, her voice breathy.

Knox wasn't sure he believed her. But he also wasn't sure it really mattered anymore.

His hands settled at her hips, fingers slipping beneath the hem of her cotton tank to find the soft skin of her belly beneath. He needed more.

And this time he had no intention of denying himself what he wanted most...*her*.

Dear Reader,

Everyone has secrets. Those pieces of our lives—and ourselves—we'd rather keep hidden. But generally when the truth finds the light of day—and it always does—the fallout isn't as bad as we expect.

When someone truly loves us, they don't see our flaws as earth-shattering and can often help us put our fears into perspective. Being vulnerable enough to share both the best and the worst of ourselves is the biggest step in any relationship.

As you can imagine, that moment doesn't come quickly for Knox McLemore and Avery Walsh. Avery's secret has the potential to destroy Knox's business and upend her world. How can she tell him the truth without losing everything that matters to her—including him?

I hope you enjoy *In Too Deep*. Be sure to return in November for the last book in the SEALs of Fortune series, *Under Pressure*. I'd love to hear from you at kirasinclair.com, or come chat with me on Twitter, @KiraSinclair.

Best Wishes,

*Kira*

# Kira Sinclair

—

## In Too Deep

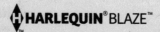

ISBN-13: 978-0-373-79856-8

In Too Deep

Copyright © 2015 by Kira Bazzel

**Printed in U.S.A.**

**Kira Sinclair** writes emotional, passionate contemporary romances. A double winner of the National Readers' Choice Award, her first foray into writing fiction was for a high school English assignment. Nothing could dampen her enthusiasm...not even being forced to read the love story aloud to the class. Writing about sexy heroes and strong women has always excited her. She lives with her two beautiful daughters in North Alabama. Kira loves to hear from readers at kirasinclair.com.

## Books by Kira Sinclair

### HARLEQUIN BLAZE

*Bring It On*

*Take It Down*

*Rub It In*

*The Risk-Taker*

*She's No Angel*

*The Devil She Knows*

*Captivate Me*

*Testing the Limits*

*Bring Me to Life*

### SEALs of Fortune

*Under the Surface*

To get the inside scoop on Harlequin Blaze and its talented writers, be sure to check out blazeauthors.com.

All backlist available in ebook format.

Visit the Author Profile page at Harlequin.com for more titles.

This book is dedicated to all of my CrossFit Protocol peeps. We sweat together, groan together and lament our sore muscles. But you guys make the worst—and best—hours of my week bearable. You've pushed me to find an inner core of strength I didn't know I had, something I've really needed over the past year. You guys rock!

# 1

"Here comes fun," Asher Reynolds taunted under his breath.

Knox McLemore fought the urge to wipe the crooked smirk off his business partner's face. At the moment Asher was making it damn difficult to remember they were also friends.

"Trouble," Knox countered. Clearly, the woman walking toward them was nothing but trouble.

From the deck of the *Amphitrite*, Trident's diving ship, Knox squinted. He didn't bother shielding his eyes from the glare of the Bahamian sun. It was a small nuisance compared to the major pain in his ass marching down the dock in their direction.

She paused, speaking with the two men toting her luggage—all six matching pieces of it. He couldn't hear her words, but even from this distance, her no-nonsense expression had his spine snapping straight. Dammit all to hell.

He almost felt sorry for the men to whom she was currently giving detailed instructions.

Dr. Avery Walsh was dressed as if she thought the bustling pier was Wall Street—perfectly tailored cream pants with a knife-edge crease ironed into each leg, a jade silk top and a cream blazer that hugged the curves of her body and buttoned just below the swell of her breasts.

If she was trying to hide the assets God had given her, she was failing. The jacket's button sparkled in the sun, some kind of stone that drew a man's eye right there…and then automatically up.

She looked tall, but that was an entirely artificial impression considering the five-inch heels she wore. How the hell did she manage to walk across the uneven boards without catching one of those spindly spikes in a crack?

But she didn't. In fact, she strode across the rough and splintered surface, staring straight ahead, with the kind of speed and purpose that drove Knox crazy.

"Come on, you're exaggerating," Asher said, a wicked grin stretching across his face and a delighted twinkle in his eyes. Bastard. "Avery isn't that bad. Her reputation is spotless and no one could argue with her expertise."

He might be right, but there was something about the woman that rubbed Knox the wrong way, and had from their first meeting several weeks ago.

It was her attitude…and the stick lodged firmly up her ass. Life was meant to be enjoyed, savored. He knew it was too damn fleeting—could be snuffed out at any moment. You had to take time to appreciate the little things while you could.

Like the gorgeous turquoise water of the Caribbean surrounding them. The sky so clear it felt as if you could reach up and touch God. And the salty, floral scent of the air filling his lungs.

They were in Nassau. Most people would kill to have the open water as their office. Would lap up the laid-back island vibe and embrace the slower pace.

But not Avery. Apparently, the doc didn't know the definition of the word *relaxed*.

She'd come into that first meeting as a whirlwind of energy and information. Obviously, she'd done her homework on the *Chimera*, the Civil War ship Trident was claiming for salvage.

But Knox had picked up on an edge of desperation behind the wall of competence and confidence she used as protection. No one else on the team had seemed to notice.

Considering the scuffle he and the doc had gotten into in the parking lot outside the Trident offices in Jacksonville, everyone had ignored his concerns.

"There you go, spouting her credentials like you've memorized her résumé. If I didn't know you better, I'd think you had a hard-on for her intellect." Knox glared at his friend.

So Avery Walsh was one of the best nautical archaeologists in the business. That didn't mean there wasn't more going on.

"To hear you and Jackson talk, you'd think the woman walked on water instead of harvesting artifacts from beneath it."

As far as he was concerned, Jackson and Asher were all blinded by hope, believing Avery was the answer to the major snag their salvage of the *Chimera* had hit.

Several months ago Jackson and Loralei Lancaster, reluctant owner of Lancaster Diving and now Jackson's girlfriend, had discovered a Civil War ship that had sunk off the coast of Rum Cay over one hundred and fifty years ago. At the time, they'd thought the biggest obstacle to salvaging the *Chimera*—rumored to carry millions in Confederate gold—would be the instability of the ship and her final resting place at the edge of an underwater ravine.

Boy, had they all been wrong.

Since the wreckage sat in international waters, they'd petitioned the US government for exclusive salvage rights under constructive in rem jurisdiction. Jackson was handling the business side of things, trying to work through the red tape that accompanied claiming and salvaging a ship with the *Chimera*'s pedigree.

Knox, on the other hand, had been eager to take on the challenge of heading up the salvage once their permits were approved. Until it'd become clear that included dealing with Avery Walsh.

They'd all been blindsided when, several months into the process, Anderson McNair had made a claim that the ship they'd discovered wasn't actually the *Chimera*, but another ship *that he'd found first*.

McNair, an American running his own diving company out of Turks and Caicos, had a reputation for cutting corners, destroying historically valuable artifacts if they had no monetary value and generally being a pirate.

Trident hadn't dealt with him before now, but Knox had asked around and none of his contacts thought highly of the man. Unfortunately, not only did McNair have enough clout and charisma to pull Trident into a media war, the man had bent some Bahamian official's ear and they were now putting pressure on the US court to pull Trident's salvage permits.

None of them knew for sure what McNair's endgame was, but they all assumed this was a play to claim the wreckage—and treasure—for his own.

Thanks to his charm and some fancy talking, Jackson had convinced all sides to let them hire an expert to authenticate the wreck. Trident was paying for Avery's services, although both governments had retained refusal rights on their chosen expert. Luckily, McNair and the judge had agreed.

Now they were racing against the clock to prove the ship was the *Chimera* before they lost everything.

He didn't dispute the fact that Dr. Walsh had a stellar résumé. However, that did little to allay his disquiet where she was concerned.

He'd be the first to admit that from the moment he'd laid eyes on her, his blood had been stirred. They hadn't exactly started off on the right foot and she'd been pissed, her gorgeous blue eyes filled with fire even as her words had remained steady and clipped. He'd seen the passion she couldn't hide and had wanted to channel it in other ways.

But it hadn't been until they'd sat across a conference table from each other that the back of his neck had begun to tighten and tingle with wariness. She'd given all the right answers. Had appeared absolutely perfect. Too perfect.

He'd made no secret that he hadn't wanted her for the job. But he, Jackson and Asher were equal partners—the three of them having served together in the SEALs before opening Trident—and he'd lost the vote.

"This is going to be damn entertaining." Asher grinned, his gaze tracking Dr. Walsh as she climbed aboard the ship.

"Tell me this isn't the only reason you're here," Knox grumbled. The woman hadn't even set the pointy toes of her pumps on his deck yet and he was already in a foul mood.

"Of course it is, man. I wouldn't miss the fireworks for anything."

"Don't you have another job to do?" Knox asked, irritation bubbling through him. This entire situation was going to be bad enough, he really didn't relish having an audience…especially Asher who would delight in rubbing the tension in his face at every opportunity.

"Yeah," Asher shrugged. "But I don't have to leave for the Great Barrier Reef until next week." Setting his back against the railing, Asher spread his arms wide and gave him a shit-eating grin that Knox wanted desperately to knock off his face.

Unfortunately, he didn't have time to swap bloody noses right now. Even if going a few rounds of hand-to-hand with his friend might drastically improve his mood.

"Thought I'd come help you out for a few days."

"You just didn't want to be locked in the office alone with Kennedy."

Asher pretended to shiver. "True. That woman could teach the Navy a thing or two about control and intimidation."

Knox laughed. He never had any trouble with their office manager. But then, Kennedy actually liked him. He had no idea what Asher had done to her, but his friend had obviously ticked her off. Staff meetings were often an exercise in veiled barbs, which could be highly entertaining since they weren't aimed at him.

"Gentlemen, if you're done swapping barbs and figuratively smacking each other on the ass, perhaps we can get to work?"

The irritated voice scraped down Knox's spine. He tossed a glance over his shoulder, even though he knew exactly who was going to be standing there.

She was just as gorgeously untouchable as Knox remembered. Every bright red hair on her head perfectly in place. Hell, the woman had even put on lip gloss. He didn't want to notice how shiny, wet and utterly kissable it made her mouth, but he was human after all.

Knox took a deep breath, preparing for the battle he fully expected. He'd faced terrorists, bombs, men with machetes and machine guns. He'd been shot, stabbed and had various body parts nearly blown off in explosions.

It had been a long time since anything or anyone had unsettled him.

Avery Walsh scared the shit out of him.

"Welcome aboard, Firecracker," Asher said.

Firecracker. It was the perfect nickname for the woman standing in front of them, and not simply because her hair was a deep, dark red, the sun popping bursts of copper off the mass pulled into a tight knot at the top of her head.

Knox didn't want to admit, even to himself, just how much he wanted to reach up and pull every last pin out of the mass just to watch it tumble around her ivory face.

Avery Walsh struck him as the kind of woman who was wound so damn tight that at the first sign of friction she could simply spark up and ignite—and not necessarily in the good way.

He much preferred women who knew how to roll with the punches and wouldn't hesitate to explore a good time. The kind who were up for any adventure as long as it had fun written all over it. Something told him Avery wouldn't know fun if it bit her on the ass, and was more likely to maintain the ice-queen persona than explode with lust.

Which was a crying shame.

Asher let his gaze travel up and down Avery's body in an open invitation that the man didn't even realize he was making half the time. It usually had women melting into puddles at his feet.

Reinforcing Knox's impression, Avery simply stared at Asher, her mouth thinning into a tight line before she completely dismissed him. "Mr. McLemore, I understand you're in charge of the *Amphitrite*."

Knox leaned back against the railing crossing his ankles. "I sure am, doc," he drawled.

"Avery." Her icy eyes snapped with annoyance. They were gorgeous and clear, unbelievably pale, which only added to the impression that she could cut you with nothing but a laser glance.

These next couple of weeks were going to be brilliant.

"Remind me to murder Jackson the next time I see him," Knox muttered at Asher out of the side of his mouth.

"Loralei might have an objection."

A few months ago, Jackson and Loralei had been at odds, racing to see who could find the *Chimera* first. It turned out they'd both won. Not just finding the ship, but each other as well.

Shaking his head, Knox pushed away from the railing, sauntering closer to the good doctor.

The self-indulgent part of him wanted to set her off-kilter. To ruffle her feathers just to prove he could. But even as he crowded close, towering above her despite the heels, Avery simply stood her ground.

Knox was the guy the SEALs had called on to crack the most difficult men, to interrogate and terrify. On the surface he might seem laid-back and unconcerned, but he'd broken some of the most stubborn and highly trained enemy operatives in the business without resorting to tactics that skirted legalities.

Dr. Walsh didn't even flinch as he came within an inch of brushing against her body. She kept her eyes trained completely on his, her face perfectly blank as she stared up at him.

"Let me know when we're finished with the pissing contest," she said, her voice smoky and even.

All right. Apparently they weren't going to dance around this thing. "I don't want you here, Doctor."

"Avery. And you made your position abundantly clear during my interview, Mr. McLemore. But here I am."

A smile bloomed across her face. What did she have to smile about? They were locked in a battle of wills, one he was beginning to worry he might actually lose.

But even as that thought flashed across his brain, her damn smile distracted him. It changed everything, taking her from remote and untouchable to downright breathtaking. It didn't just brighten her face, the twinkle in her eye revealed the first insight he'd gotten into how she ticked.

She was enjoying this, even if she'd never admit it. Getting off on the tension and antagonism between them.

Interesting.

"Just so we're both clear on where we stand," he said.

The corners of her lips lifted higher. "I know exactly where I'm standing—on the deck of your ship. So I guess I win."

Knox couldn't stop his own lips from twitching. "For now."

It bothered him, her flat-out determination to be a part of this project, even in the face of his obvious lack of enthusiasm. That only made more warning bells clang deep inside his brain.

Why had she pushed so hard to be involved, to the point of contacting Jackson several times even after meeting with the Trident team? Was it simply ego and a drive for another line on her résumé, or was there something more behind her eagerness?

His instincts told him it was the latter, he just couldn't prove it. Yet.

Cocking her head, she said, "In a few hours we'll be in the middle of the Caribbean. I don't think you can change the status quo by then, especially considering you lost that fight the first time around, but feel free to try."

INSIDE, AVERY WAS a quaking mess. She was bluffing, but then most of her life had been a bluff.

The problem was, this time someone was waiting to call her on it.

Anderson McNair had her trapped and there was nothing she could do about it.

Almost six weeks ago he'd walked into her office and informed her that he knew her little secret and if she wanted it to stay just between the two of them she was going to help him. Remembering that day made her stomach churn with anxiety and guilt.

Anxiety and guilt she'd been fighting for years.

It didn't help that Knox McLemore intimidated the hell out of her. Not to mention that he could set her body on fire with nothing more than a scorching gaze.

From the moment he'd nearly run her over with his shiny black speed demon of a car—in the Trident Diving parking lot, no less—she'd wanted to hate him. But she'd needed to win the job more, and not simply because working on the *Chimera* was the kind of project she lived for.

If she failed and they hired someone else, Anderson McNair would ruin her reputation and sink her business.

Part of her had hoped Trident would award the project to someone else. Then the years of wondering and worrying would have been over.

But her life wasn't the only one poised to be ruined. Her sister, innocent in the entire situation, would suffer as well. And Avery couldn't stomach that.

McNair expected her to sabotage the assignment… to torpedo her integrity and announce that the wreckage wasn't the *Chimera*, no matter what the evidence proved.

Her only hope was that Jackson Duchane was wrong and the ship they were heading toward really wasn't the *Chimera*.

Best-case scenario—but her life never worked that way.

Avery couldn't worry about that right now, though. She needed to concentrate on getting through the next five minutes without Knox McLemore realizing how vulnerable to him she really was.

A feral smile crossed his face. "Let's get one thing clear, doc."

She hated that word. And not simply because Knox seemed to delight in shortening her professional title. That got under her skin plenty, but she preferred no one use it…because she hadn't actually earned the damn thing.

"You're on my ship. I make the rules."

Knox studied her with a slow, lazy perusal that had lightning shooting beneath her skin. She'd already been sweltering under the pounding tropical sun, but suddenly sweat slicked every pulse point on her body.

She wanted to reach up, unbutton her blazer and sling it off. The only thing that stopped her was knowing the layer of linen was all that kept her tight nipples from Knox McLemore's sharp gaze.

McLemore was the kind of man she stayed far away from—mellow, confident, purposely provocative. Because despite the persona she'd developed for business, inside she was still the shy, quiet girl who'd spent years moving from place to place and never quite fitting in anywhere.

Just standing in front of him left her edgy. She wanted to take a step back, but her feet were frozen in place.

She couldn't seem to tear her eyes from Knox's faded, ripped jeans and the T-shirt clinging to his powerful muscles. His dark brown hair was too damn long, flopping into his eyes in a way that both frustrated and enticed her.

She wanted to take a pair of scissors to it at the same time her fingers itched to pull it back so she could see his eyes. When it was in the way, it was difficult to know what he was thinking. Something that made her even more nervous.

Her skin itched. Her body throbbed. He was in her personal space and she wanted to break the connection, but her limbs simply wouldn't respond.

Asher cleared his throat, finally breaking the spell. Relief rushed in when he said, "Why don't I show you to your quarters, Firecracker?"

Avery graced him with a tight, grateful smile. "Thanks."

She was hot, tired and sticky. Getting out of her travel-stained clothes sounded like heaven.

She turned to follow Asher, but unfortunately Knox kept pace behind them. She could feel the heat of his hot caramel eyes sweeping up her back.

"You know these allegations are bullshit," Knox said from behind her.

This was even ground, arguing with him about the job. "No, I don't know that, Mr. McLemore. And I'm fairly certain you don't either. There's enough doubt that the judge was ready to rule against your request for diving rights."

"And enough evidence that they agreed to wait for further verification," he said, each word lazy and sure. She didn't know which she hated worse, when he was intentionally antagonistic or when he seemed smugly certain her presence here was a waste of everyone's time.

Unfortunately, he wasn't wrong. She'd read the research presented by the Trident team. She'd followed the detailed information on just how Jackson Duchane and Loralei Lancaster had come to find the wreckage. She had to admit their case was strong, but whatever evidence McNair had provided was enough to cast doubt...not that she necessarily thought it valid.

But Knox didn't need to know that.

"She's the *Chimera*, doc."

Avery gritted her teeth, resisting the urge to correct Knox again about the damn nickname. He was doing it on purpose now, which drove her insane. But she wasn't willing to play his game.

"That's what I'm here to find out, Knox." In the cramped hallway, she stopped, turning to face him. Better to deal with this now than later. "This whole process will go much smoother if you get out of my way and let me do my job. We both want the same outcome."

Knox reached out, as if he was going to touch her arm, but stopped just short of actually doing it. They both stared at his fingers just hanging there in the empty space between them.

"I'm not entirely certain that's true."

She tried not to let his distrust panic her. "Why do you say that?"

Knox pressed closer, invading her personal space without actually touching her. The pressure of anxiety and awareness weighed on her chest, making it difficult to pull in a full breath while she waited for his answer.

Only he never gave her one. Instead, his lips pulled up into a smile that wasn't real.

"I'll have your bags sent down, doc."

# 2

SEVERAL HOURS LATER they were finally underway, heading for the open sea. Later than Knox had wanted because of a few logistical snags…including hauling all six of Dr. Walsh's suitcases onto the ship.

Had the woman packed her entire wardrobe? What did she expect to need on a ship in the middle of the Caribbean?

He'd thought about opening every one of her bags and rifling through—with the intent to toss any heels, pearls or matching pantsuits he found along the way—but had decided his blood pressure probably couldn't take the exercise.

Besides, he'd figured his time would be better spent looking for something that would tell him what she was hiding. Although, he didn't do that either.

Avery had disappeared into the cabin she'd been assigned, which she had to herself despite their already cramped quarters since the only other woman on the ship, their cook, had quarters right off the galley. So far, she hadn't resurfaced. Not even for dinner or to meet the crew.

They were all going to be working together for the next

few weeks. The least she could have done was introduce herself and pass around a smile.

Trident had been open for a little over two years, but even though they were a relatively new business, and quite a few of the crew had only recently been hired on, they were a tight-knit group.

Maybe it was a legacy from their time in the Teams, but Asher, Jackson and Knox had worked hard at building camaraderie and a sense of family with their employees. As soldiers, they'd depended on each other for their lives. While they no longer worked with bullets flying, you had to trust that the guy beside you knew what he was doing and could competently and quickly complete his job, freeing you up to do the same.

They worked hard, and they played hard. When jobs required 24/7 commitment and living in tight quarters, it was sometimes just as important to blow off steam together.

Rather than wallow in irritation, Knox had come up on deck to try and calm down. The quiet shush against the hull as the *Amphitrite* cut through the water would normally have been enough to accomplish that. But not tonight. What he really needed was a spin behind the wheel of his Shelby, but that wasn't in the cards.

Tonight he was restless, the first time he'd felt that way since leaving the Teams. Somehow, after living through more life-and-death situations than he cared to count, not even the stress of owning his own business made him uneasy.

There was something about this whole adventure, though, that didn't sit right with him. Not just having Avery aboard. But the allegations McNair was making.

In his gut, Knox knew this was an attempt to grab their work. This had to be McNair's play to claim the wreckage and treasure for himself. When Trident had announced that the *Chimera* had been found, there was a frenzy of interest, rumors of gold heading for the Confederate States a huge media draw.

They'd already been approached by a documentary crew from a major science channel interested in recording the process of salvaging and preserving the wreckage. Kennedy was currently working to get the details for that project in place.

McNair was simply one of the sharks that had swum out of the depths.

But unlike the others, he was causing serious problems.

Knox wasn't going to let McNair's claims derail their plans for the *Chimera*. And, unfortunately, Avery Walsh was a major part of solving the issues plaguing them. So he needed to take Asher's advice—bite his tongue around the maddening woman and let her do her job.

While keeping a sharp eye on everything she did.

The sooner she completed her task, the sooner she could be off his ship. And the sooner they could get back to business as usual. He could return to the uncomplicated existence he'd enjoyed for the past two years.

That was what he wanted.

Uncomplicated. Unhurried. A life doing what he'd come to love—spending his time in warm, tropical waters—with two of his best friends.

After the turmoil of the past sixteen years, he deserved a break.

Knox stared out across the vast expanse of open water. It was calm, smooth this far from any shore. It always managed to make him feel small and insignificant. For some people that might be frightening, but for Knox it was reassuring. Knowing that he was one teeny, tiny piece in a gigantic whole helped to take some of the pressure away. Not everything was his fault or responsibility.

Sometimes that lesson was difficult to remember.

As he usually did whenever the stars winked on for the first time at night and he happened to be in a position to see them, he looked up. Picking one out, he closed his eyes and murmured a few words to his big brother. About his life, his day—good and bad.

He was so caught up in the moment that he didn't hear anyone approach until a soft voice murmured beside him.

"They're beautiful, aren't they?"

Jerking his gaze down, Knox stared for several seconds at Avery.

She wasn't close. There was at least three feet of railing between them. Although it didn't matter. His body reacted as if she'd whispered those words straight into his ear, as if the warmth of her breath had tickled across his skin.

Knox tamped down his reaction, controlling it as he'd learned to ruthlessly control everything else. Desire, just like pain, could be ignored.

And he had every intention of ignoring any reaction Dr. Walsh stirred within him.

At some point she'd changed clothes, probably into what she considered casual wear. Sure, she was in shorts, but they were linen and looked damned expensive. She'd paired them with a gauzy top in fading shades of blue and fussy sandals with straps that crisscrossed up her calves. And the damn pearls—although this strand was longer than the ones earlier, and swayed between her breasts.

She'd pulled her flame-red hair up into some kind of bun thing at the back of her head that managed to look both sophisticated and complicated. Not to mention tight enough to give her a headache. Knox just wanted to mess it up.

For the briefest moment, he contemplated whether or not to tell her a few strands had escaped the tight confines and were curling to trail down her neck and face. He decided not to, mostly because he knew she'd immediately try to tame them back.

As far as he was concerned, those wisps of red were the best thing about her outfit.

"What?" he finally asked when he realized he'd been staring at her a little too long.

"The stars, they're gorgeous. It's one of the best things about being on the open water. So bright. No matter where my family was, or how foreign our home felt, the stars were always the same. I could look up into the sky, and even from our first night in a new city or village, I'd feel centered."

Her statement struck him as sad, wistful in a way that tugged at him. And curious.

"You moved a lot?"

She laughed, the sound soft and uneasy. "Every few months. My dad was an archaeologist but my parents liked having the family together, no matter how remote the location."

Shifting her hips against the railing, Avery rested her weight there. She stared out across the quiet water.

Knox didn't quite know what to do with this contemplative version of the woman he'd met. So he stayed silent and simply listened.

"My sister and I were homeschooled. My parents wanted the world to be our classroom, and I have to admit there were things about the experience I wouldn't trade. But for someone who tended toward shyness, it became very difficult to dredge up the energy to make friends in each new place."

Knox studied her, wary instincts clanging a warning deep inside his head. What was her angle? Was she playing him? Doling out information he hadn't asked for in the hopes of tugging on his heartstrings—assuming he had any, of course?

Like any good intelligence officer, he let her continue in the hopes of discovering the answer to some or all of those questions.

"My sister and I would often wish on the first star of the night. But I suppose that would be too foolish for a big, bad Navy SEAL, huh?"

"Doc, I think you've got the wrong impression of me. There have been plenty of times in my life I would have prayed to wood nymphs, Aztec gods or, hell, Martians, if it meant saving lives. I believe in my training. I respect the brothers who fought beside me. And I'm wise enough to realize there are forces at work outside our control every single day. I value life and understand what's important—people, not things."

Her pale blue eyes jerked to his. "Interesting."

"What?"

She shrugged. "Just not what I expected."

Knox felt his lips curve down into a frown.

Slowly she cleared her throat, turning and folding her arms over the railing so she could stare down at the water churning beneath them. "Look, I think maybe we got off on the wrong foot."

"Maybe?" There was no question they'd gotten off on the wrong foot.

"Hey, you're the one who almost ran me over with that little car."

"Doc, that wasn't just any car. And she might be small, but she's damn powerful."

"And fast."

Knox grinned. "And fast."

He mirrored her position, sliding closer and folding his own arms over the railing.

"What's so special about the car...aside from the fact that it came inches away from wearing me as a hood ornament?"

He could have rattled off a bunch of statistics, talked about the car's racing history. Instead, Knox found himself saying, "First of all, like I told you that day, I was in complete control the entire time. You were never in any danger."

"Excuse me if I don't trust your judgment on that."

Knox's lips flashed up into a self-deprecating grin, the kind that acknowledged her statement and then immediately dismissed it. Because she was absolutely wrong. However, he was intelligent enough to realize that having this argument again wasn't going to get either of them anywhere.

"But, more importantly, it's my brother's."

Which wasn't true since Kyle had never owned it, but Knox always thought of the car as his. It should have been his.

Kyle had talked about that car incessantly. Had put posters of the Shelby on his wall. Together, the two of them had planned to fix one up. His brother had even started saving.

Since Kyle hadn't been able to follow through on the dream, in his spare time Knox had done it for him. It had been a labor of love, and of atonement. It was the least he could do since Kyle's death had been his fault. That car was Knox's single most prized possession.

The familiar guilt snaked through his chest, tightening everything to the point that he couldn't breathe. It was a battle he'd fought for the past sixteen years. A battle that never seemed to get easier.

It didn't matter that no one else blamed him for the accident that had killed his brother, his brother's girlfriend and his best friend. He blamed himself and always would.

He should have done more. Not swerved to miss the deer that had jumped out onto the dark country road late that night. He should have been able to recover from the skid the car went into. Should have prevented the car from slamming into the guardrail at sixty miles an hour.

Everyone told him it was a miracle he'd walked away from the crash. And they weren't wrong. He'd had several broken bones, a concussion and various cuts and bruises.

Bethany had died on impact. Chase minutes later on the side of the road. Kyle…he'd survived for several hours.

Knox would never forget standing beside his brother, watching EMTs try to save his life. The most helpless Knox had ever been. A sensation he never wanted to experience again.

"Your brother needs better taste in cars."

Pushing away from the railing, Knox let his gaze sweep across Avery. "My brother's dead," he said, his words blunt and infused with every drop of remembered pain, even if he hadn't meant to unleash it on her.

Avery's pale eyes went wide and her mouth dropped open.

He should feel…something for pulling that kind of reaction. Satisfaction, at least. It was what he'd been going for with the stark statement.

Instead, he simply wanted away—from her and the unpleasant memories she'd unwittingly called up.

Turning, he walked in the opposite direction, leaving her with the pod of dolphins that had decided to ghost through the water with the ship.

KNOX'S WORDS RANG through her head. Okay, more like clanged. But how was she to know his brother was dead? Or that her question could cause that haunted, hunted look in his eyes?

She felt like crap, but there wasn't much she could do about it. Apologize, but she'd really done nothing wrong. And something told her saying anything else would make the situation worse. It was obvious he didn't want to talk about it.

She'd seen Knox standing at the railing looking up at the stars and had wanted to get things on track. She really needed Knox to…if not like her then at least leave her alone enough to do her job. Or not do her job.

At the thought, a heavy pit settled into her stomach. It made her sick. Instead of making things better, somehow she'd managed to irritate him more.

It was clearly time to regroup.

Avery headed back to her cabin. She'd been surprised to be assigned her own considering the lack of space, but it would make things easier. She was exhausted from traveling and her body was starting to crash from the ups and downs of the day.

She forced herself to unpack—the cases with her supplies and equipment had already been unloaded—putting all of her clothes away before beginning her nightly ritual. There was something about getting her space in order that always soothed her.

Maybe it was from all the years living out of suitcases. Or a holdover from trying to find a sense of security when the only thing she'd been able to control was her immediate environment.

Her father's work had taken them to some amazing places—Africa, Egypt, Thailand, South America, Australia. She'd experienced different cultures. Could understand five languages, though she wasn't fluent in all of them.

She now owned a house in Texas, but she spent more time away from it—consulting, working, giving speeches or preparing papers, occasionally teaching—than there.

While she liked it well enough and always enjoyed going back, she wasn't tied to home the way most people were.

Her routine grounded her, though. No matter where she laid her head, it was always the same. Brushing her teeth, taking off her makeup, preparing her clothes for the morning...

She could barely keep her eyes open by the time she switched off her light and crawled beneath the blanket. Tonight she didn't even bother cracking open the book she'd brought with her. Instead, she was asleep within minutes.

And awake again two hours later when a loud noise startled her.

Avery jackknifed straight up in bed, her body responding before her brain had fully kicked in. With bleary eyes, she glanced around, trying to figure out where she was and what had woken her. It only took a few seconds to realize the disturbance had come from outside her room. On the *Amphitrite*.

Loud music. Laughter. Someone yelling.

And, there it was, the thump of some idiot slamming into the wall in the hallway outside her door.

Throwing a silk robe on over the cotton shorts and tank top she normally wore to bed, Avery yanked open her door just as another down the hall slammed shut. At least the drunken fool had made it to his bed.

But the noise. In the hallway it was so loud, the ship practically vibrated to the thump of the music.

She'd never get back to sleep.

With a huff, Avery tightened the knot on her robe and headed toward the commotion. A door down the hall stood wide-open. Inside it appeared the entire crew had congregated.

The space wasn't huge. The ship was a working vessel, so most areas onboard were needed for their mission. It was clear this room served multiple purposes. The crew had eaten their dinner there earlier in the day. Now everyone was scattered about—lounging in chairs, sitting on top of tables, playing poker, drinking beer, listening to music.

Someone, she'd guess Catherine, their cook, had put out several bowls of munchies and a few dips.

Everyone's faces were bright with happiness and laughter. She stood on the edge of the group and for a minute jealousy twisted her gut. She'd never had this, not even at college.

Especially not at college. She'd been too young and shy to really fit in with the other undergrads. Graduating high school early, she'd started college at sixteen.

By the time she'd reached grad school, she was so focused on her goals and burned-out that trying to fit in had seemed like a lost cause. She'd simply drawn into herself and set her sights on completing her program as soon as possible.

She had a few close friends now, but they were people like her. Quiet, professional, contained. When she was in Galveston, they'd get together for dinner, wine and some conversation. Nothing like this.

Avery's gaze swept across the sea of people, most wearing shorts, T-shirts and flip-flops. There was nothing about this group that said *contained.*

They looked like they were relaxed. Enjoying themselves. A bright spurt of envy bloomed inside her chest.

Shaking off the unproductive reaction, Avery reminded herself why she'd ventured out. Scanning the crowd, she tried to find Asher. Maybe he'd be willing to tone down the party so she could sleep. He'd seemed like a nice enough guy the couple times they'd met.

But instead of finding him, her gaze locked with Knox's. From across the room she felt the unexpected zing. Once she saw him, she couldn't seem to look away, even though her brain was screaming at her to.

Pushing away from the table he'd been leaning against, Knox set his bottle on the scratched surface. Then he was striding across the room toward her. He didn't have to say anything, the people between them simply moved out of his way.

"Welcome to the party. Have to say I'm surprised you joined us." His dark eyes studied her. "In your silk robe."

Avery fought the urge to grab the lapels and pull them tighter over her chest.

Luckily, his words jump-started her brain and reminded her exactly why she was there.

"Would you mind turning down the music? I'm trying to sleep and it's very loud."

"Sorry, doc. I promised the crew a party tonight since we're going to be pulling twelve- and fourteen-hour days once we get to the site."

The party. The music. The nickname. Having this man stare down at her out of those smooth brown eyes, delicious and warm…it was wreaking havoc with her brain. Why did she always have the impression Knox was judging her?

And why did it bother her so much that she was afraid he didn't like what he saw?

Frustration piled up, making her response more explosive than she'd meant. "For the love of all that is good and holy, *stop* calling me that."

Knox considered her. His head tilted to the side and the tip of his tongue snuck out, slowly sweeping across the firm edge of his lower lip.

Avery's stomach rolled and heat leaked into her veins, spreading unwanted desire like poison through her system. She should have stayed in bed.

She shifted on her feet, ready to turn away and admit defeat. Maybe she'd just put her earbuds in and hope for the best.

But Knox snagged her arm before she could move two steps. His fingers wrapped around her bicep, sliding against the silk covering her skin. "Ever heard the phrase, 'if you can't beat 'em, join 'em'?"

A low groan rumbled through her chest. Avery's eyes slid shut as she asked for strength in dealing with the man. "Never mind."

Knox shrugged, that damn grin twisting his lips even as his eyes began to twinkle.

Without asking he reached into a cooler and came up with a beer bottle. Water and ice slid down the smooth glass. Knox didn't seem to care that it left a puddle on the floor at his feet.

He cupped his palm around her hand and sent a flame of awareness shooting up her arm. Slapping the bottle against her palm, he curled her fingers around the ice-cold surface. "You look like you could use this. If nothing else, it might help you sleep."

Avery blinked at him, speechless.

Her brain, the thing that had faithfully served her for years, revolted. So her body took over, raising the bottle to her lips and pulling in a huge swallow. She didn't particularly like beer, preferring cosmos and wine. Tonight, she didn't even taste the liquid pouring down her throat.

Asher sauntered up to the two of them. Where the hell had he been a minute ago when she'd needed him?

He grinned at her, his eyes flashing mischief and mayhem. Whatever he'd sauntered over for couldn't be good.

"Interesting wardrobe choice, Firecracker."

Asher wasn't the first person to give her that nickname.

Her bright hair made it an obvious choice. Why couldn't Knox have latched onto it instead of *doc*?

"Her beauty sleep was disturbed," Knox said, his tone ripe with laugher. "Although I have to admit I like the robe better than the pearls, heels and business suit."

Avery's shoulders straightened and she wished she'd thrown on a pair of those heels so she could look him in the eye when she glared at him.

Being five foot four was often a hindrance, especially in the male-dominated field of nautical archaeology.

When she'd first started her career she'd wanted to eliminate at least one disadvantage when dealing with older male colleagues who tended to dismiss a young female out of hand. Heels and professional clothing had been her solution. And, over the years, had sort of become her signature. In her mind, projecting a competent, conservative image could never be a bad thing.

But apparently Knox McLemore didn't see it that way.

"Hmm," Asher murmured, taking a pull on his own beer. His gaze drifted down, lingering at the V where her robe closed. There wasn't any heat in the perusal—it was more like it was a habit. "You do realize that just makes me want to find out what you've got on underneath, right?"

"Stop sexually harassing our employees, Ash. We're going to end up with a lawsuit." Knox frowned, his lips pulled into a tight, thin line.

A little-boy grin curled across Asher's lips, his eyes sparkling with mischief. Avery realized Asher wasn't playing with her, he was intentionally riling up Knox. Which was fine with her. The man deserved some of his own back.

Drawing another sip from her beer, Avery casually mentioned, "Technically, I'm not your employee."

The corners of Asher's eyes tipped up a little higher and

his smile went to megawatt. "Does that mean I'm free to sexually harass you?"

Avery opened her mouth, but Knox beat her to it. "No, no you are not."

"Doesn't bother me," she answered.

Asher chuckled, clinking the neck of his bottle against the one she still held in her hand. Then he winked and sauntered away. Avery watched him, not with lust, but fascination. She'd never had that kind of confidence.

"Stop staring, doc. Trust me, you don't want to go there."

"I didn't…I don't…" she sputtered, finally slamming her mouth shut.

Wrapping a hand around her arm, Knox led her through the room to the table he'd been propped against when she walked in. He settled his hips back against the edge. She did the same.

"Stay. Mingle. Have a beer. You're going to be part of the team for the next couple weeks, Avery. It's probably a good idea that you get to know the crew."

The way he said her name, his low, smooth voice caressing each syllable, sent a jolt of something twisting through her. Was it the first time he'd actually used her name? She thought maybe it was.

She liked it a hell of a lot better than *doc*.

"I don't need to braid hair, have a pillow fight or sneak beer from my parents' fridge in order to bond with your team, Knox. I'd hope your crew is professional enough to do the same. No one has to like me in order to do their job."

"No, you're right. No one has to like you. It would make things easier, though. On everyone."

They sat there, the weight of their silence, in contrast to the laughter and music surrounding them, pressing in on her until she had to say something.

"It's not that I don't want to be a part of the team. I'm not very good at bonding with colleagues."

She should have felt anxious about making the confession. But there was something about Knox—while he usually made every muscle in her body tighten with tension, at the moment he'd somehow managed to put her at ease.

"That sounds…depressing."

They sat there for several minutes. Avery watched as the people around them laughed. Why couldn't she be that way? Why couldn't she feel comfortable socializing like this?

Out of nowhere, Knox reached out and snagged a strand of her hair, running it between the pads of his thumb and forefinger. "Something tells me you worry too much. I like your hair down."

The unconnected thoughts had her brain spinning. Or maybe that was the beer.

His hand continued down, the backs of his fingers brushing against the edge of her robe.

"Ash isn't wrong. I'm dying to know what you've got on under this thing. Want to hear my guess?"

Avery swallowed. She did and she didn't. She could take Asher flirting with her because she wasn't attracted to him despite his charm and good looks.

But she didn't think she could take Knox messing with her. Already she could feel the tide of blood rushing to the spot where his finger had brushed against her skin.

Somehow she found the strength to shake her head. Unfortunately, for some reason, the word, "Yes," tumbled out of her parted lips at the same time.

Something mischievous flashed through his dark eyes, joining the dangerous grin that tugged at his wicked mouth.

"Well, judging by the rest of your clothes, something

silky. Lots of lace. Probably in some soft color like pink or baby blue."

Her voice was breathy, but not nearly as shaky as it could have been, when she responded, "I hate to disappoint you, but I'm wearing cotton shorts and a Texas International University tank top."

His grin widened. "Now why would you think that would disappoint me? Actually, I like the idea of that a hell of a lot better than the lingerie."

He leaned closer, his lips near enough that she could feel the heat radiating off his skin. His scent welled up around her, a combination of musk and salt and man.

His low, quiet voice rumbled in her ear, "Gives me hope that deep down, beneath that perfectly polished surface you prefer to show the world, there's a real woman."

Breath caught in the back of her throat. Heat and longing flooded her system. Her fist tightened around the bottle in her hand, needing something to hold on to so that she wouldn't reach for him.

And then he had to go and ruin the moment.

Knox murmured, "Sleep tight, doc," before walking away, leaving her alone, breathless and seriously turned on.

Bastard.

# 3

"You know we can't trust her, right?"

Up on deck, the early-morning air seeped beneath his thin T-shirt, making goose bumps pearl across his skin. The sun, rising low in the sky, flowed off the smooth surface of the water surrounding them. It was funny how mornings like this could remind him of similar moments he'd spent in the desert, the light glaring off sand instead.

Knox, cradling a steaming mug of coffee in his hands, shot Asher a sharp glare. "Pretty sure I said that weeks ago, right after we interviewed her."

Leaning against the railing, Asher raised a single eyebrow. "Yeah, but you said it because you have a problem with her. I'm saying it because something about this whole thing stinks."

"Oh, you mean like McNair slithering out from whatever rock he lives under to claim the wreck isn't really the *Chimera*?"

"He wants the gold. And apparently he's got enough connections to make a play. I don't trust McNair."

No joke. The man was slick and charming. The kind of perfect that made you think the veneer could crack at any moment to reveal the truth underneath.

"Avery and McNair are connected."

"So you noticed the inordinate amount of glee McNair was woefully inept at covering when we announced she'd been hired?"

"Oh, yeah. And the way, after weeks of delays, the Bahamian government agreed to the US court's decision, letting the paperwork sail through the minute Dr. Walsh signed on to the project."

Knox had put two and two together, coming to an answer he didn't like. For multiple reasons. He'd called in several favors, but none of his contacts had been able to find a concrete connection between McNair and Avery. It was there, though. He just knew it.

The whole situation left him uneasy. As if he was walking into hostile territory with no idea which direction the bullets might fly from.

Something about Avery worked under his skin, itching and irritating until he wanted to pick at it. Pick at her. Annoying her could quickly become his favorite hobby out here on the open sea with nothing else to occupy his time and mind.

It was either that or crowd her against the closest hard surface and kiss the fire out of her. Something he'd nearly done last night.

That damn robe she'd been wearing was designed to entice a man. The way it had brushed against the tops of her bare thighs, clung to the curves of her breasts…and the fact that she hadn't put it on for that reason only made the appeal more difficult to ignore.

He'd had a hard time reconciling the vision of the woman who'd shared a beer with him and the professional, put-together executive type who had walked on to his ship hours earlier.

Avery was competent, intelligent and good at her job.

But last night he'd realized she was also more complex than he'd thought and surprisingly introverted.

He was still struggling with that revelation. Considering their first encounter had involved her yelling at him for his stupidity, he would have expected that to be the last adjective he'd ever use to describe her. There'd been nothing shy about her that afternoon.

And while he'd been attracted to the cool, collected Avery, something about the small chink of vulnerability she'd revealed last night made her even more appealing.

It had been difficult walking away from her.

Knox was blaming his reaction on the three beers he'd indulged in before she arrived. Although he hadn't even had a decent buzz going.

From his vantage point across the room, he'd watched her walk out, the roll of her hips a metronome begging him to pursue. But he'd forced himself to stay put and enjoy the party with his crew.

Asher leaned against the railing, pulling Knox back into the conversation. Hell, the woman wasn't even here and she was distracting him. This wasn't good.

"All I'm saying is you should drag out those rusty surveillance skills to keep an eye on her. Or, hell, that charm you're famous for. I've noticed it's been decidedly AWOL since Dr. Walsh arrived."

"There's nothing rusty about my skills," Knox said, popping Asher in the shoulder.

"Keep her close." The twinkle in Asher's eyes and his lifted brow clearly suggesting just how he thought Knox should accomplish that objective.

"WE'RE JUST RUNNING sonar to ensure the wreck hasn't shifted since the last time we were down. Given what happened to Jackson the first time he entered the *Chimera*—"

"If she is the *Chimera*," Avery interjected. Knox ignored her, although the way his eyes narrowed at the edges suggested her statement had registered.

"—there's really no reason for you to come with me."

He had to be joking. There was no way she was letting him close to that wreck without her. Who knew what the cowboy might decide to do if she wasn't there to rein him in? He said he had no intention of going down, but once he was on that boat away from the ship, she had no guarantee.

"Not a chance in hell."

"Suit yourself, doc."

Avery refused to rise to the bait. He was doing it on purpose, but she was going to be the bigger person.

They loaded the sonar equipment on to one of the smaller boats the crew kept. A half an hour later they were heading out to the location of the wreckage.

And Avery had to admit to the bubbling euphoria rippling through her chest.

She loved her job. It was amazing to help recover and preserve pieces of history that had been lost for ages. She'd seen pictures of the wreckage, haunting as it stood silent and still beneath the water.

But there was no way the photos could be as impressive as the site itself. She wanted to see it. The need was a physical pressure inside her chest, that drive to be down there with the memories and history so perfectly preserved by the cold, dark water.

There was nothing like the peace she always found beneath the surface. Something that often eluded her up in the air.

The *Amphitrite* was anchored quite a way from the site for safety reasons. They wanted to be well clear of the wreckage so that they minimized the potential for disturbances, especially since she rested so close to the edge of the ravine and had already shown signs of instability.

They were going to have to get closer eventually, but for now protocol dictated they visit the area as little as possible. They approached the site, Knox throttling down as he turned the sonar equipment on and began to take readings of the seabed beneath them. She had enough experience to read the data spilling back at them and identify the dramatic depth difference where the rocky ledge the *Chimera* rested on dropped off.

Her heartbeat sped as the outline of the wreckage appeared on the screen. Slowly, the equipment revealed what had brought them both there—proof that a sunken ship sat over a hundred feet beneath them.

Excitement and impatience buzzed through her system, making it difficult to sit still. She wanted to be down there, not stuck on the small boat with Knox.

Avery found herself holding her breath in a mix of anticipation, excitement and guilt.

No, she wasn't going to go there. She had no idea if the ship below them was really the *Chimera* and until she did there was no sense in borrowing trouble.

Avery watched Knox work, grudgingly admitting that he knew his way around the equipment. Even if he moved at a snail's pace while using it. Every shift of his body was deliberate—the way the muscles in his arms and legs rippled as he moved, adjusting knobs, flipping switches, staring at the readout.

The longer she sat and watched him, the more tension seemed to fill her body. The boat was small. The man was big. And he wouldn't let her do anything.

"Let me help."

"No," he said, without even bothering to look up from the data.

"Come on. I'm just sitting here."

"I told you it was pointless for you to come, but you insisted." The *so sit there and be quiet* was implied by his tone of voice.

Avery didn't appreciate that much either.

Her fingers began tapping on the edge of the boat, a rhythm she couldn't seem to stop. She wasn't used to watching someone else work. Being idle drove her nuts.

After several minutes, Knox finally threw her a glare. "Stop that."

Beneath the weight of his gaze, Avery stilled. For a moment. And then she deliberately thrummed her fingers against the smooth wood again.

It might have been childish to enjoy watching the edges of his mouth tighten with irritation. But there was a part of her—a bigger part than she really wanted to admit—that delighted in knowing she could get under his skin the same way he managed to dig at her.

"Payback is hell," she taunted.

Knox opened his mouth, she expected a string of unhappy words to flow out, but instead a slow smile bloomed across his face. It crinkled the corners of his eyes. Light and laughter flashed through them, turning the caramel color to something hot and inexplicably making her mouth water.

Leaning sideways, Knox dipped his hand into the water beside them. Cupping his palm, he scooped up a handful. Avery knew what was coming, but there was nothing she could do. Nowhere to go.

"Don't you—"

He did, flinging the salt water straight at her. It cascaded down the front of her shirt leaving splotches over the cotton. Droplets clung to her eyelashes and the wisps of hair that had fallen down from her ponytail.

"You're right, doc, it sure is."

Avery wanted to yell at him. She opened her mouth to do it, but nothing came out. She wasn't used to men playing with her. Didn't know how to react. Especially since her entire body was responding as if he'd touched her instead of the water, flaming hot and throbbing in inopportune places.

At least she could blame her tightened nipples on the cool breeze drying her shirt.

Out of nowhere, a low buzz interrupted any retaliation she might have planned. At first it was faint enough that Avery thought maybe Knox had stuffed his cell into his pocket. But as the sound grew, the rumble quickly increasing to a whine that vibrated through her chest, she realized that wasn't the case.

Then a small plane appeared on the horizon.

"Knox," she said, pointing to where the speck was quickly growing.

It wasn't unusual to see planes carrying passengers or cargo from island to island, but this one was out in the middle of nowhere.

"It's coming in low," Knox murmured, almost to himself. Abandoning what he'd been doing, he straightened, using a hand to shield his eyes from the glaring sun. "Very low."

He flipped an assessing glance at her. It didn't last more than a few seconds, but it was enough to let her know he somehow thought she was responsible for whatever was happening.

What the hell?

The plane buzzed past, banking hard to the right and swinging in a large arc. At a diagonal, it headed away, but managed to drop even lower in the sky.

"What the heck are they doing?"

"McNair."

It wasn't an answer, and yet it was. "You think he's surveying the wreck site?" Surprise crept into her voice, although once the words were out of her mouth, she didn't know why.

It was exactly the kind of thing McNair would do. Even thinking he had her firmly lodged in his back pocket, he wasn't the kind of man to leave things to chance.

Or maybe he was just checking up on her.

Anxiety ricocheted through Avery's rib cage. He needed to back off or he was going to ruin any chance she had of doing what he'd ordered.

Then something tumbled out of the back of the plane and plunged toward the water.

"Oh, my God!" Avery shouted, shooting to her feet. The boat rocked unsteadily with the sudden shift in weight. Knox reached for her hand and tugged, pulling her back down.

As they watched, a parachute popped free of the dark spot plummeting toward the water. Avery let out a sigh of relief, slumping onto her seat.

The dangerous descent slowed. Whatever had fallen dropped out of their line of sight, but there was no doubt it had hit the water.

Knox barely gave her any warning before revving the engine. "Hold on." He cranked it high and jolted forward, speeding in that direction.

Gripping the edge of the boat, Avery closed her eyes against the spray of water whipping into her face. The boat bounced on the waves, sending her stomach jolting up and down between her throat and toes, until she felt as if her insides were jumbling together. Adrenaline surged into her already spinning system.

It didn't take them long to reach the object, five minutes at the most. But the *Amphitrite* was no longer on the horizon. They were surrounded by nothing but open sea on all sides, which normally wouldn't bother her.

Except someone had dropped something into the water and the parachute suggested it was intentional.

For the first time since everything had started, Avery began to question why they were chasing after whatever it was.

A huge wooden box came into view. The parachute stretched out across the water like a colorful oil slick. On all sides were inflated tubes keeping the cargo afloat.

Avery was getting a really bad feeling.

"Uh…remind me why we raced over here?"

Knox flashed her one hell of an untamed glance. It had the pulse fluttering in her throat with a mixture of lust and excitement.

"Because, doc, I'm a SEAL and we don't run from trouble, we barrel toward it."

"Fabulous, but could you do that when I'm not around?"

His mouth hardened, but he didn't respond. His focus was entirely on the box in front of him. He slowed the boat, circling the box, stirring up a wake that rocked both it and their boat.

Knox maneuvered close and then cut the engine, floating the rest of the way until the side of their vessel bumped gently against the roughly hewn wood.

"It's probably a drug drop."

Avery's eyes slid closed, her stomach clenching tight. Not the words she'd wanted to hear, but not altogether surprising. "Then we should leave and call the Coast Guard or something."

"Coast Guard doesn't have jurisdiction out here."

"Then let's call whoever does."

Knox was shaking his head before she'd even finished

the sentence. "By the time they get here this shipment will be long gone."

"But they'll know where to look next time."

He ignored her statement. "Do you see that?" He pointed to a tiny object affixed to the side of the box toward the top. "Homing beacon."

Beautiful. So whoever was coming to pick up the box had a device to lead them straight there. "So we're just going to what, wait for them to show up? Knox there are two of us and we're unarmed."

"I know," he said, his voice tight.

Jumping in front of the wheel, Knox cranked the engine. He scanned the horizon, even as he began to maneuver away.

"Hang on. I'm getting us out of here."

Avery's knuckles turned white as she gripped the edge of the seat. Her heart pounded so fast she could feel the whoosh of blood as it sped through her veins. She wanted the boat to be going just as fast.

But before Knox could steer them away, a loud humming sound rolled across the water. Unlike the plane, it didn't build quietly but went straight from low to roar.

A black boat streaked across the water, heading straight for them like a bullet.

"Dammit," Knox breathed out.

Avery felt her eyes widen with fear and disbelief. How had her day gone so completely sideways? They were supposed to be playing with sonar, not dealing with drug runners.

The boat approached quickly. Low and sleek, it cut through the waves at a speed that boggled the mind. It screamed up beside them, throwing spray that coated her skin in seawater and sandwiching their vessel against the box.

The engine cut out suddenly, and a lazy drawl came from the other boat.

"You appear to be lost."

The man speaking had bronzed skin and gleaming white teeth, along with an American accent, insolent smile and sharp eyes. He stood in front of a group of men who didn't bother to hide the guns pointed in their direction.

Avery glanced over at Knox. Gone was the guy who'd splashed water on her earlier, slapped a beer into her hand last night and made inappropriate comments about her sleeping attire.

The person glaring at the men in the boat next to them was a soldier. One who'd put his life on the line multiple times and would do so again to protect his friends and family. Maybe even her…

A shiver of awareness and apprehension rocked through Avery's body.

Knox's jaw was tight, his eyes alert and watchful. But none of that came through in the languid words that slipped through his lips. "That's funny, I was going to say the same thing about this box. I'm guessing you're the owner."

The leader shrugged his shoulders. "I am."

Moving carefully, Knox positioned himself so that he was in front of her, making himself a target for the weapons trained their way.

"Well then, I suppose it's a good thing you showed up to retrieve it. Saves me the effort of hauling it back to my ship."

The guy on the other boat laughed, throwing his head back as if Knox had just told the most amazing joke. The sound grated against Avery's already frayed nerves.

This was not going to end well.

And there was nothing she could do about it. She was

trained in Muay Thai, something she'd begun when her family lived in a small village in Thailand during one of her father's archaeological digs. But that skill was useless with them occupying separate boats. Muay Thai required close contact…their guns, not so much.

That didn't stop the adrenaline from flooding her system. Or the involuntary way her body adjusted, muscle memory taking over and preparing her for a fight she really didn't want.

Her movement caught the drug runner's attention. Shifting on his feet, he peered at her around the wall of Knox's body. The grin he sent her was wolfish.

She'd seen that expression before, on a different face. One she tried not to think about because that night had altered her life…and her sister's.

But there wasn't time for those memories right now.

Standing slowly, Avery filled her voice with determination and said, "Take the cargo and let us leave."

The man's grin widened. "I think it's adorable you believe you have any say in what's going to happen next."

$$4$$

THE MINUTE KNOX had pulled up to that crate and seen the tracking beacon, he'd known they were in trouble. He'd hoped to get away, but feared they wouldn't have time.

A drop like this...the guys waiting to retrieve it wouldn't be very far away.

What the hell had he been thinking, chasing after an object falling from the sky with an untrained civilian along for the ride?

But the reality was the *Chimera* site was too close to the drop. He might have avoided a confrontation today only to stumble straight into another one later, with more people caught in the crosshairs and a ton of expensive equipment on the line.

He'd made the best choice he could given the circumstances, but that didn't ease his conscience when there was a gun pointed straight at Avery's head. These men were seasoned professionals. Knox recognized the workings of a well-oiled team.

Grim regret pulled at him. When they got out of this, he was going to owe Avery.

On the bright side, she'd surprised him. He'd half expected her to dissolve into hysterics. Instead, she was glaring at the men in the opposite boat. Okay, so he could have used a little less attitude from her—because he wasn't the only one picking up on her hostility. But he'd take what he could get.

His legs shifting beneath the easy rocking of the boat, Knox really wished he could feel the reassuring metal of his Beretta against his palm. It had been a long time since he'd missed that sensation.

He'd have to make do with the wrench he'd taken from the toolbox under the seat along with the emergency beacon he'd surreptitiously stuffed into his pocket before the other boat had arrived.

"Sweetheart," the leader said, "why don't you jump on over here."

It was a command, not a question. And Knox seriously disliked the predatory expression that accompanied the words.

"Don't move, Avery," Knox countered, even as she started to obey.

"What? Really?" She froze and a little spurt of relief shot through him. Not that it lasted long.

The leader smirked, his lips twisting. "That looks like some pretty expensive equipment."

"It is," Knox said slowly, grinding the words out.

"Here's what we're going to do." Turning to one of his men, the leader gestured at their boat. Before Knox could move to block him, the guy crossed, planting both feet aboard their boat.

"Miguel is going to escort your pretty friend over here. Then, you're going to follow."

"Why would I do that?"

"Because if you don't, Miguel will put a bullet in her brain."

Miguel smiled, the kind of psychotic grin that told him

he not only wouldn't hesitate to pull the trigger, but would enjoy it.

Knox had run into enough men like him in his career to recognize a sociopath when he saw one. And these men were all cut from the same cloth. They weren't just in the business for the money, they enjoyed the rougher side of life that came with drug running.

He ground his teeth. They were outnumbered and outgunned. His best bet for protecting Avery was to do as he was told...for now. None of the men realized he was a SEAL. Had the training to take them out, if they'd just give him a small opening.

It was clear he was being underestimated, but that had always been one of his greatest assets...allowing him to blindside his opponents and leverage the power of surprise.

People genuinely liked him, often accepting his easygoing outlook on life at face value. For some reason, most people automatically trusted him. A quality that had made him an excellent interrogator.

Knox watched, helpless, as Miguel wrapped his hand around Avery's arm and lifted her across the expanse of water into the opposite boat. She stumbled over the edge. Knox lurched forward, intent on helping, but before he could reach her one of the other men had a gun buried against his shoulder.

"How sweet," the leader drawled.

At gunpoint, Knox followed, constantly scanning for an advantage he could use, but there was none. They were outnumbered and outgunned.

Miguel pushed him onto the backseat, forcing Avery down beside him. Thank God for small miracles, no one bothered to tie them up. Not that it made much difference, since two of the men still had guns trained on them.

From his position, Knox watched them hook a three-point line onto rings that were already anchored in the wooden box. The third man took the controls in Knox and Avery's boat.

Knox had to bite his tongue when the man sped off, taking with him some damned expensive equipment. Losing it hurt. But not nearly as much as getting shot or watching Avery bleed would have.

Out of nowhere, Avery's hand landed on his thigh. She squeezed. He wasn't sure if the gesture was supposed to be a warning or reassurance. Either way, it worked because he felt his blood pressure slipping back down to something more manageable.

She wasn't scared. Or was damn good at hiding it if she was.

"Are you okay?" he murmured, low enough that the whine of the boat engine would cover up their conversation.

She nodded. Loathing flashed through her eyes as she glanced at the men holding them hostage. That was good and bad. He appreciated her spark, but only to the extent that she could control it. The last thing he needed was for her to open that smart mouth of hers and land them in even more trouble.

"Keep a grip, Avery. Don't do anything stupid."

She glanced at him from beneath her lashes. "What's your definition of stupid?"

*Oh, shit.*

THAT FIRST SURGE of adrenaline faded, leaving Avery shaky and angry. The men standing guard didn't waver, not even as their boat bounced over waves. The dark eyes of those barrels stayed trained on them.

The longer they sat, the more tension she could feel winding through Knox's body. The rock-solid curve of his thigh pressed her leg. Each time the boat surged over a wave his wide shoulder brushed against hers.

At first, she'd been praying they would make it out of this alive. But after she'd calmed down and realized that if the man in charge had wanted them dead, they'd both be sinking beneath the surface of the Caribbean Sea right now, she'd switched her focus. From that point on, she'd prayed Knox wouldn't decide to play hero and do something that would get either or both of them shot.

About an hour later, dread dropped into her belly. She watched as a land mass materialized out of the unbroken blue. It didn't take long to notice they were heading straight for the tiny island instead of passing by.

"Knox," she whispered.

"I know," he murmured back.

Suddenly, the reasoning she'd used to convince herself they were going to be okay wasn't nearly as sound. Was this where they were going to die?

The boat sped up to the island, curving sharply about fifteen feet from the shore. As abruptly as they'd approached, the engine was throttled back. They idled, floating sideways, carried by their wake for several moments.

Turning, the leader flashed them a pointed look. "This is where you two get off."

Avery looked over at the island. It was quiet and clearly deserted. "You have to be kidding."

The corners of the drug runner's lips curled. "I'm not. Nor am I completely cruel. Miguel will follow with a few supplies. Matches, rope, alcohol."

"You're all heart," Knox said.

"He's been watching too many pirate movies," Avery muttered.

Another one of those roaring laughs erupted from deep inside the criminal's chest.

"So glad I could entertain you," Knox said.

"You're going to have your hands full with this one, my friend."

"I'm not your friend."

The smile disappeared in a flash, making Avery realize just how much of a lie it had been.

"No, but you're going to be smart and not start anything. I'm leaving you both alive."

Knox spread his thighs and planted his feet firmly on the bottom of the boat. Avery could feel his muscles bunching, preparing for whatever was coming.

"And why is that?"

The corners of his eyes twitched, indicating that whatever he was about to say would likely be only half the truth. "You said yourself, I'm all heart. But if you push me, I'll have no compunctions about leaving you on this island with a bullet wound while you wait to be rescued. And you will be, eventually.

"This island might be deserted now, but fishermen come by here on a regular basis. It'll only be a day or two before you're discovered. Enough time for us to be long gone."

Avery could feel the frustration flowing off Knox's body. It was ratcheting up her own tension to the point that she wanted to scream. And if she'd thought it might help she would have done just that.

But she was afraid it would upset the tentative balance and cause a chain reaction that would end with bullets flying.

So, instead, Avery stood. Knox turned, glaring at her.

"We'll go quietly."

Miguel followed, using the business end of his gun to indicate she should throw her leg over the side of the boat and jump into the water. She did as she was told, sucking in a sharp breath as the water rose to just beneath her chin.

Heading for shore, she didn't even hear a splash as Knox entered the water, but before she realized what was happening, his strong arms were stroking through the waves right beside her.

As she reached the shoreline, Miguel growled out an order in heavily accented English. "On your knees."

She threw a glance over her shoulder. Miguel used the barrel of the gun in his hand to wave her back around. Avery's heart lurched inside her chest. Wasn't this usually how drug dealers killed people? At least, it always was in the movies.

Slowly, she sank, the warm sand coating her wet knees and calves. It was soft and welcoming. Any other time she might have appreciated the pristine stretch of beach. At the moment all she could think about was the injustice that it was potentially going to become her final resting place.

Knox dropped down beside her. Twisting her head, she scanned his face. It was drawn and hard, his mouth grim. He stared straight ahead into the line of trees several yards away up the beach.

Something brushed her fingers where they hung uselessly by her side. Suddenly, they were tangled with his, gripped tight. He squeezed, giving her a moment of comfort before pulling away again.

A bundle smacked the ground off to their left.

"Do not turn around until you hear the boat engine or you will both die."

Avery swallowed and squeezed her eyes shut. Waiting.

Behind them, the boat's engine revved higher. Avery twisted in time to watch the sleek, black machine shoot away.

They were alive, but stranded. Not ideal, but it could be worse.

Popping to her feet, she took several steps back toward the water, watching the retreating boat.

Knox slipped up beside her. His arm circled her shoulders, pulling her against the shelter of his body as they both stared out across the now-empty water.

"We're going to be fine."

"How can you say that? We're alone on a strange island. No one knows where we are. Hell, I don't even know where we are."

He laughed, honest to God laughed. How could the man find anything funny right now?

"Neither do I, but it doesn't really matter." Reaching into his pocket, he pulled out a small device. "Underwater locating beacon like the ones attached to a plane's black box. Each of the Trident launches is equipped with one in case the boat sinks. I grabbed it before the others arrived. It might take a while for Asher to realize we've gone missing and start searching for the high-frequency sonar pulse the device puts out, but he'll be here eventually. We just have to stay safe until that happens."

He made it sound so simple.

Avery walked up an incline. At the rise she could see down to the other side of the island.

They'd rounded the long stretch of land on their way in, so while she knew it was about a mile and a half long, it wasn't very wide. The middle of the island was covered in thick trees and brush. It might be small, but it was definitely big enough to hide snakes, spiders and various other creatures that might be curious about the newcomers.

"Sure, stay safe. We don't have shelter. Or food and water."

"Maybe not, but we have alcohol," Knox said, lifting the bottle of clear liquid high in his fist.

Joy of joys.

With a self-deprecating smile, he dropped it onto the sand at his feet. Rifling through the rest of the bag, Knox tossed several energy bars, a book of matches, rope and a rather wicked-looking machete down beside it.

Avery didn't understand his frown. At least they weren't going to starve before Asher showed up. Hopefully.

"Why are you frowning?"

"Because none of this makes sense."

Dropping beside their pile of supplies, Knox settled back, legs sprawled and elbows digging into the sand. He stared off across the water, his eyebrows beetling together.

"Why didn't they kill us? Or just let us go in the first place? And why provide us with a bag of supplies?"

"You heard him, he didn't want us contacting the authorities before they could get away."

His hot caramel eyes swept across her body, starting at her toes and working up until he connected with her eyes. "How many drug dealers have you known?"

His tone implied he already knew the answer. The problem was, he didn't.

"More than you probably think."

His eyebrows rose. Avery sighed, pulling her own gaze away from his. She really didn't want to get into her history, but it wasn't like they had anything else to do on this island.

Dropping to the sand beside him, Avery didn't sprawl as he had. She folded her legs neatly and began sifting the soft sand through her fingers. The motion was soothing somehow.

"My sister was a drug addict. She liked to date dealers because they'd keep her supplied for free."

"Was?"

Out of that entire statement, he'd picked up on the past tense and decided that was most important?

"A little difficult to remain an addict when you're confined to a hospital bed. Although, I suppose if you really want to get technical, Melody is still an addict, the drugs are just legal now."

"I'm sorry." His quiet words were meant to be soothing, and, really, she appreciated the sentiment. But she hated when people apologized for what had happened to her sister. It was Melody's fault.

Well, Melody's and her own.

If she had handled things differently that last night, maybe her sister would have been home where she belonged instead of attempting to drown her misery with an almost-lethal cocktail of drugs and alcohol.

"Don't be. Not your fault."

Knox hummed, the sound full of understanding and support, something she didn't want to need. But a warm feeling began to bloom in the center of her chest. Maybe he was simply being polite, but Avery didn't think so. And Knox's sympathy mattered.

"Where is she now?"

"She lives at a care facility in Galveston. She sustained brain damage from an overdose. With hard work and dedication she's managed to recover some of her speech and motor function, but not enough to take care of herself."

Avery stared at the grains of sand slipping through her fingers as she thought about Melody's life. Her sister had been so vibrant and outgoing. Where Avery had been shy, people had been drawn to her sister.

Melody was the artistic one, finding an outlet in drawing, painting, creating. Avery had been happy to sit quietly in a corner, reading about ancient civilizations.

Her sister was all emotion and explosion while Avery had been contained and logical.

But she'd loved her big sister. Had looked up to her. Wanted to be her. Envied her on so many occasions as she'd watched Melody put on skimpy clothes that highlighted her tanned skin and amazing figure, clothes Avery would have been too self-conscious to ever think of wearing.

She didn't envy Melody now. She hated when other people pitied her sister or stared at her with regret for the life wasted, but Avery thought the exact same things every time she looked at her, and that always made her feel guilty.

Avery could feel the weight of Knox's gaze on her, but refused to look at him. She didn't want to see the expression of grief and sympathy she knew would be there.

She didn't deserve it.

Slowly, he reached for her. Avery's breath caught as his fingers brushed against the soft skin of her thigh beneath the tight cuff of her shorts. She stayed still, unsure whether she was afraid to spook him and have him stop, or unwittingly encourage him to do more.

But apparently sitting still didn't make a difference. His caress went higher, skimming over her hip, the curve of her arm, to the warm hollow of her throat.

"What exactly do you do for fun, doc?"

This time, when he used the nickname, it didn't sound like a taunt, but an extension of his caress. The soft, low rumble rolled across her skin just as surely as his touch.

"Fun?"

"Yes, fun. Outside of your work, what do you do to unwind?"

Avery shook her head, unable to think of anything that would provide a suitable answer. She had hobbies. She had interests outside her work. She just couldn't think of any at the moment. No woman could with Knox McLemore touching her that way.

The pads of his fingers slipped up her throat, rolling across the surface of her pearls and making the smooth orbs slide against her skin. The sensation was…maddening and unexpected.

She'd worn them almost every day since her parents had given them to her for her college graduation. They reminded her of everything she'd accomplished, the price for her drive and success. If she let her focus slip, even for one minute, it could all come crashing down…like it had for Melody.

Like it would for her if she didn't come through for McNair.

The silky-smooth texture always grounded her. Reassured her. Not once had they ever felt sensual against her skin. Until right now. When Knox stroked across them, rolling them against her skin, something else happened. She felt…energized. Electrified.

Avery wasn't sure that was a good thing. In fact, she was pretty certain it wasn't.

And, yet, she couldn't pull away. Knox watched her, his warm gaze glued to her throat. She couldn't breathe. Her arms, legs and lungs refused to move.

One corner of his mouth tugged into a lopsided grin, the little-boy one he'd been taunting her with since the day they met.

Knox shifted closer, the heat from his body reaching out to touch her. A shiver rocked her, sending a cascade of tingles sparking through her system.

Oh, hell.

Avery's lips parted. Her mouth was dry. She needed a drink. She needed…him to kiss her and make her forget the predicament they were both in.

Maybe he was a mind reader.

His eyes flared, dilating. The warmth of his palm curved around her neck, urging her closer. She expected wild and unruly, like he was. Instead, what she got was gentle and coaxing. The soft caress of his breath as he whispered her name right before kissing her.

God, it was good. Every nerve in her body trembled at the contact, wanting more. She might have sighed. She definitely fisted her hands in his shirt trying to pull him closer.

And then reality hit.

She didn't want this. No, she *shouldn't* want this.

Pushing him away, Avery scrambled backward, sending up a flurry of sand as she tried to escape the mistake she'd just made.

Knox let her go, simply watching with that knowing, steady stare of his. He didn't even bother to wipe the sheen of moisture her abrupt end to their kiss had left.

Avery tried to ignore the heavy throb of need pulsing through her body with each pump of blood.

After several moments, Knox quipped, "That's definitely my idea of fun." Without waiting for a response, he pushed to his feet. Avery couldn't help but notice the way his body moved with tight grace and barely leashed power.

"I'm going to see if I can find us something more substantial to eat on this little stretch of land we're going to call home. Why don't you start gathering wood to make a fire?"

He didn't even bother waiting for an answer before sauntering off. Without breaking stride, Knox reached down and scooped up the machete, tossing it back and forth between his palms in a way that made her apprehensive. The idiot was going to cut himself.

"You know, there's no hospital on this island, Knox. You might not want to toss the wicked knife around."

He turned to face her, continuing to walk backward without even watching where he was going.

The little-boy grin had returned, along with a glitter of mischief lodged deep inside his eyes.

"What? You're not willing to kiss it and make it better if I get a boo-boo?"

What would she do if the idiot hurt himself?

Frowning, she jumped up from the sand and charged after him.

"You're not going anywhere without me."

# 5

THEY'D BEEN TROMPING around the island for twenty or thirty minutes and Knox still couldn't get the taste of her out of his mouth. Or erase the soft sound of her breath catching in the back of her throat.

That kiss. Hell, it was like nothing he'd ever experienced. Soft and sweet, but somehow still full of heat.

He'd wanted more. But she'd pulled away and he'd always been the kind to respect when a woman said no, even if she didn't actually use the word.

"I'm pretty sure I've already seen that tree with the funny-looking knot on the side."

Knox glanced at the tree, biting back a groan. She was right.

His head wasn't where it should be—focused on their survival—but back at the beach where he wanted to stretch Avery out across the sand and see if her skin was as smooth and supple as it looked.

What was it about Avery that drove him so nuts? That had his brain scrambling from just sixty seconds of her mouth touching his? She infuriated and energized him at the same time, a dangerous combination, especially given their current predicament. "We need to find fresh water."

He heard the frustration in her voice when she said, "I think we can rule it out here, then. Maybe we should move on to another part of the island."

His mouth cracked into a self-deprecating smile. "No joke."

He watched her out of the corner of his eye as she moved through the thick brush beside him. She didn't hesitate to slap at branches and spiderwebs. She simply charged ahead, determination stamped on every feature.

He knew men who, faced with their situation, would lose their shit at least for a few minutes. Avery hadn't done that at all. Not even when there was a gun pointed at her head.

She'd earned his respect today, that was for damn sure.

"Look. I don't know how long it'll take Asher to find us. While the beacon will help, he has to be within a certain range to pick it up."

Avery made a little grimace of concern.

"He'll get here," Knox was quick to reassure her, "But for now I'm going on the assumption that we might be on this island for a little while."

"Little while as in a few hours or little while as in a few weeks?"

God, he hoped it wasn't a few weeks.

It had been difficult enough on the *Amphitrite* to keep his distance. On the ship there were plenty of crew members and lots of work to keep him occupied. But with just the two of them and the reality of that kiss… He was afraid it was only a matter of time before his control snapped.

They walked for several more minutes, heading into the middle of the island. The increased vegetation made Knox hopeful. Plants and trees needed water to survive as well.

Maybe it would be better to clear the air, get everything

out in the open and talk about what had happened instead of letting it fester.

Knox stopped. Avery slammed into him.

Before she could so much as rock backward on her feet, he reached to grab her. Twisting them both, he pressed her back against the closest tree, searching for balance he wasn't sure even that solid surface could provide.

Not when she was so close.

She gasped. Her eyes widened and her luscious pink lips parted. The pulse at her throat fluttered.

"Are we just going to pretend that didn't happen?" he asked, his voice thick and husky.

He should move away now that she'd found her footing. But he couldn't. Instead he shifted, closing the gap between them.

She hadn't bothered with makeup before they'd gotten into the launch this morning. Her skin was luminous, even more beautiful now that it was free from the artificial crap women seemed to think necessary. The warm Caribbean sun, sinking down behind the trees, brushed her cheeks as she stared up at him.

She licked her lips, rolling them in and swiping the tip of her pink tongue across the plump surface.

Knox bit back a groan. Was she torturing him on purpose?

"Pretend what didn't happen?" Her voice was breathy, the sound of it scraping against his good intentions.

"That kiss."

Avery closed her eyes for the briefest moment before opening again…only this time he could see the heat she couldn't quite hide.

He watched her draw in a single, heavy breath.

"Yes, let's pretend it didn't happen. It was a mistake. We're working together, Knox, even if you didn't want me here. This is a difficult situation and we don't need to make it any more complicated."

She swallowed, her throat working. She was right. Knox knew it, but his body didn't seem to care. He wanted to bend his head and run his tongue across her creamy skin. To suck on the pulse point fluttering just beneath the surface.

Goddammit.

He took a step backward, away from her, away from temptation.

Blindly, Knox spun and stumbled farther into the dark green foliage surrounding them. After several seconds, he heard the softer tread as Avery followed.

Gritting his teeth, Knox reached deep for the calm he was famous for. He had to find it again, for both their sakes.

"I want you here. Sure, you irritate the hell out of me on occasion, but that just keeps life from getting boring."

She made a sound, a cross between a snort and a laugh. It was unexpected and somehow adorable.

"You have a real problem with boring, don't you? What is it with you and excitement?"

"You have a real problem with letting loose, don't you? What is it with you and obeying the rules?"

She shook her head. But he could see the twitch of her lips as she fought a reluctant smile.

He was so focused on her that he didn't even notice what was in front of him until his foot splashed down into a small pool of water.

It rose up to his ankle. He didn't bother moving back to dry ground, but crouched down, scooped up a handful and held it to his face. It didn't smell like salt water, but there was one sure way to know for sure.

Pursing his lips, he was about to take a taste when

Avery's hand slapped across his, spilling everything in his palm back into the pond.

"What are you thinking? That could be filled with bacteria or worse."

Straightening, Knox frowned at her. "I'm well aware of that."

"Then why were you about to drink it?"

"To make sure it was freshwater."

Little lines pulled between Avery's eyebrows.

"Surely there's a better way."

"Fine, we'll boil it. Would that make you feel better?"

"Much."

Unfortunately, they only had one container they could use and it was currently full of alcohol.

But that was easily remedied.

THE SUN HAD begun to slip behind the horizon by the time they'd gathered enough wood and tinder to start a fire. It would be dark soon, too late to head back to the pond even if the bottle had been empty.

The morning would be time enough to deal with their need for water.

Avery sat on her heels, watching as Knox struck a match, holding the tiny flare of light against the perfect stack of wood.

She fidgeted, running sand through her fingers, crossing and uncrossing her legs. She couldn't sit still.

Not having anything to do was unusual for her. She couldn't remember the last time she'd really been idle. When she was growing up, her parents had always praised her hard work. In college the other students had seemed to sneer at her tendency to overachieve. No one liked it when the seventeen-year-old ruined the grading curve.

What was she supposed to do with herself?

The fire flared between them, a burst of red-orange light that slipped across the edges of Knox's handsome face.

Digging into the bag, he tossed her one of the energy bars. "Eat this," he said before taking one for himself. "I'll work on a spear tomorrow so I can catch some fish. Maybe you can hunt up some coconuts and check for other fruit trees."

Her stomach growled. The idea of fresh fish and fruit made her mouth water. Until that moment she hadn't realized how hungry she was, her brain too preoccupied with other matters to listen to her body.

Avery unwrapped the bar, took a huge bite out of it and couldn't stifle a groan of pleasure.

Knox laughed, sprawling out across the sand. "I don't think I've ever heard anyone react that way to a meal-replacement bar."

"Not even in the middle of a shitty mission?"

"Nope, not even then. Food was necessary, something required to fuel our bodies and keep us moving. Nothing more."

"How…practical." She watched his own bar disappear in three bites. He crumpled the wrapper and tossed it into their pack.

He sat there, staring into the fire. Relaxed. Why couldn't she be that way instead of a tightly wound ball of useless energy?

Avery couldn't take her eyes off his face. The man had a beautiful mouth. She remembered the feel of it against hers. Pleasant. Unhurried.

That was the way he always seemed. He'd be the kind of lover to take his time. Draw out the experience. Nibble and tease.

Or maybe he'd be overwhelmed by passion. She'd seen

that harder edge beneath the fun-loving guy he showed the world. Would his mouth crush hers? His tongue swipe against her lips, demanding entrance?

She seriously had to stop thinking about kissing him again. It didn't matter how he kissed. She didn't want a repeat performance.

Knox leaned on one elbow, his legs stretched out, ankles crossed as he stared at her over the flames.

He was relaxed. Even in the middle of their predicament, he was relaxed.

Avery envied him that. It was a skill she'd never managed to acquire.

Her ankles were crossed as well, but positioned in front of her, knees drawn to her chest with her arms wrapped tight around them.

Tension filled the space between them, so thick she could practically taste it. There was nothing comfortable about the silence, especially with Knox watching her, his eyes drowsy and yet still somehow intent.

She wanted to look away, but couldn't.

Night fell quickly, dusk bleeding easily into darkness while they'd eaten. And now they were alone on a tropical island.

In the distance, she could hear the nocturnal creatures beginning to stir. They scurried through the underbrush, rustling limbs and leaves. The shush of the water rubbing rhythmically against the sand was unexpectedly soothing.

A cool breeze blew off the water, carrying the briny scent of salt water mixed with a touch of some sweet tropical flower. She shivered, digging her feet deeper into the sand, searching for the last vestiges of warmth the sun had left before disappearing.

For the first time, Avery wondered why she wasn't more

scared or upset. It wasn't as if she really knew Knox well. But there was something honorable about him, or maybe she was just projecting values she assumed any former Navy SEAL would have.

Still, she knew Knox wouldn't let anything happen to her. He'd stepped between her and the business end of a gun today, without thinking twice. Which was crazy, considering how volatile their short relationship had been.

After a few minutes Knox moved, rummaging inside their bag of supplies until his hand emerged, fist tight around the neck of the glass bottle.

The criminals had certainly left them an eclectic selection of supplies. But she guessed they'd simply pulled from their own stash.

She supposed there was no use in contemplating the minds of those who made their living running narcotics. Still, she couldn't help but wonder why they'd left her and Knox alive, much less provided them with supplies.

The pale liquid sparkled in the firelight.

Avery wasn't much of a drinker. She'd never been the frat party kind of girl, especially after watching her sister's struggle with addiction.

However, if there was any situation that called for a little liquid relief, this was it.

Standing, Knox rounded the fire and lowered himself to the ground beside her. His thigh brushed against hers as he stretched across the sand.

"We might as well enjoy this." Twisting off the cap, he tipped the neck toward her in salute and then pulled a huge swallow before offering the bottle to her.

She reached for it, trying to ignore the fire that erupted up her arm as their fingers tangled. It would soon be drowned out by another burn anyway.

Grasping the bottle, she couldn't help but grimace at the sharp scent as she brought it close to her mouth.

"Bottom's up, doc," he said.

Her lips wrapped around the smooth edge. Liquid flames poured down the back of her throat. She didn't even really taste it, but the inside of her nose suddenly felt as if it was on fire.

"What the hell is that?" Avery wheezed. Setting down the bottle, she sucked in hard, trying to catch her breath. "That stuff is awful."

Knox gave her a twisted, lopsided smile. "Moonshine. Apparently, they're multitalented criminals.

Jeez, the stuff was vile, but even now Avery could feel the pleasant warmth spreading from her belly out to her fingers and toes.

Her entire body tingled, as if she'd been standing just a little too close to a lightning strike and conducted the residual charge.

The second swig wasn't quite as bad. By the fifth she couldn't taste anything.

Back and forth, they silently shared sip after sip. It didn't escape her notice that her sips were much smaller than Knox's, although that made sense. He was a big guy, all shoulders and arms and thighs to die for.

After a few drinks her body began to relax. Pretty soon it felt as if the moonshine had replaced her muscles. She was all liquid warmth and firelight.

It felt good. It felt strange. A relief to let the weight of everything she'd been holding up for so long just... disappear.

She loved the way the golden-red flames danced across Knox's skin. He'd taken his shirt off while lighting the fire and hadn't bothered to put it back on. She could see every curve and dip of his pecs and abs.

The man might be out of the military, but it was obvious he hadn't used that as an excuse to let his body go.

He was gorgeous. And the way his muscles bunched and flexed when he moved...

"Doc, you keep looking at me that way and we're going to do something we'll both regret."

"What?" she asked, forcibly jerking her gaze up from Knox's chest to his eyes. His hot, molten-caramel eyes. She could just lick him up with a spoon. Which was funny because she rarely allowed herself to indulge in sweets. Things that were bad for her. Just as Knox McLemore would be if she let him get too close. "What? How am I looking at you?"

"Like you want to run that gorgeous mouth all over my chest."

"Hmm." She enjoyed the sensation of the sound in her mouth. "Maybe I do."

She could hear her own words, a little slow, a little slurred. Logically, she realized what that meant, but she no longer cared.

"You're drunk, doc."

"That's usually what happens when one drinks alcohol, smart guy."

Flopping back onto the sand, Avery stretched her legs out to her side and somehow found her head propped against Knox's thigh.

She stared up at him, his head haloed by the black sky and twinkling stars. They both seemed so far away—Knox and the heavens.

He watched her, the spot right between his eyebrows creased with worry even as the corners of his mouth tipped up in stifled amusement.

Lifting her hand, Avery smoothed the tip of her finger over the ridges, hoping the action would take away the emotion causing them as well. She didn't like seeing Knox upset.

"I don't think you're drunk, though," she finally said.

"No."

"Pity. I've never gotten drunk and made bad decisions. Yet another rite of passage I've missed. Was hoping you were drunk enough that maybe we could make one together."

He made a sound, a cross between a laugh, a wheeze and a groan. "What kind of bad decision did you have in mind?"

"Oh, you know, giving in to the sexual tension that's been clawing at us both since the day we met. But I guess you're not drunk enough yet to want me."

The frown lines were back, only this time the grooves were deeper.

"No, no, no," she said, trying to make them disappear again. But her hand never connected with his face. Instead, his fingers circled her wrist, holding her just out of reach.

"Trust me when I say I don't have to be drunk to want you, Avery."

She made a scoffing sound. "I call bullshit. You don't even like me."

Slowly, Knox lowered her hand to her side. The solid weight of his thigh shifted beneath her head. She wanted to roll just a little so that she could press her mouth against him, even if his skin and muscles were covered by his clothes.

His other hand smoothed across her face, fingers gliding from cheekbone to forehead to chin in a soft caress that had a shiver rolling through her body.

"I like you just fine, doc," he whispered, his voice gruff and smoky. "You're irritating."

"Oh, yeah, that sounds like affection."

"And gorgeous and brilliant and maddening and you have a body built for sex."

Avery pulled in a gasp.

"All lush curves and compact energy. Don't doubt for a second that I want to stretch you out and touch every inch of you. I want to watch you completely unravel. I want to muss up that perfect exterior and drive you so crazy that the only thing you can think about is screaming my name as I finally give you the relief you're craving."

Avery arched her back. She couldn't help it. The sound of his voice, the words he was spilling across her like warm honey. She wanted everything he was saying. Right now. Needed him to move his hand and touch her. Soothe the tight ache of her erect nipples and the liquid burn settling between her thighs.

He growled low in his throat. His palm landed on her belly, spreading wide and applying the slightest amount of pressure. "I'm fighting very hard right now to do the right thing, Avery. Be still.

"What if I don't want you to do the right thing?"

She felt the slight tremor in his hand against her belly. The commanding force of him weighing her down. And she needed that right now. She was half-afraid that if he stopped touching her, she might simply float off into the night and never find her way back.

"I don't take advantage of women who are inebriated." His words were harsh, but his eyes glowed as they stared down at her. Devoured her.

Never in her life had she felt so…desired. And she wanted that. Wanted him.

Hell, didn't she deserve a little bit of what Knox McLemore could give? She'd been good her entire life while her sister had gone out and partied. She'd never let herself go there, because she'd seen the devastation left in the wake of bad decisions.

Avery had no doubt this was a bad decision, but for the first time she understood how Melody could be lured into them. Because there was no doubt in her mind this was going to feel good. Damn good.

"Let me tell you something, Knox. I'm not the kind of woman who does this."

"Does what? Gets stranded on a tropical island with a guy she barely knows?"

"Sleeps with someone she doesn't intend to have a relationship with. I'm the kind of woman who employs a six-date rule."

"Six? I thought most women went with three."

"Exactly," she said, throwing her hands into the air and nearly smacking Knox in the face. He laughed and ducked. And the way his hand moved across her belly… his fingers brushed the underside of her breast, leaving behind a hunger for more.

How could this man completely undo her with such an innocuous and fleeting touch while every other man she'd let into her bed had had to work damn hard for every orgasm she finally succumbed to?

"You might have noticed I'm a little uptight."

"No," he said, laughter filling the single word.

"Bastard. I don't allow myself this kind of thing." His fingers were back at her face, smoothing across her skin in a rhythm that was probably meant to be soothing, but only had the molecules inside her moving faster and faster. "But I want it now. With you. Please."

Avery was absolutely certain that in the morning she'd

hate herself for that single word and how close her voice sounded to begging. But right now, she didn't care.

"Please," she whispered again, just to make sure he understood she really meant it.

# 6

GOD, SHE WAS ADORABLE. Who would have thought perfect little Avery Walsh would be such a cute drunk? He would have bet money she'd become weepy and emotional, the alcohol finally letting free everything she was so careful to keep bottled up.

And, he supposed, that was what was happening. Lust was definitely a response, even if it wasn't the one he'd expected.

But holy hell, she was gorgeous. Her dark red hair was spread across his lap, gilded with firelight, her creamy skin luminescent as moonlight spilled across her. And those pale blue eyes…they were going to be his undoing.

So earnest, so much heat and need.

It hadn't taken him long to realize the ice queen was an act, a facade she used to keep people away. What he hadn't realized was just how tempted he would be when she finally dropped the walls.

He needed to get her out of his lap before she noticed how hard his dick was and how close to the edge of reason he teetered.

"Please," she whispered, the single word ghosting across her ripe, pink lips.

It went against every rule he lived by to even contemplate giving her what she wanted. And yet, here he was, thinking about it anyway. About how smooth and soft her skin would be. How hot and wet he could make her and how good it would feel to slide his aching cock deep inside her.

"Dammit," Knox murmured, right before his hands wrapped around her arms, pulling her close.

His lips slipped across hers, teasing. A bare brush that had her chasing after more. Avery sighed, opening her mouth to him and unconsciously giving him everything.

And it was sexy as hell, the way this buttoned-up woman with the prickly exterior just…let go and gave herself to him. It felt like a gift.

Knowing her the way he was beginning to, he realized it *was* a gift. He hadn't needed her to tell him she never did this kind of thing. So he was going to cherish what she was giving him.

Wrapping an arm around her back, Knox arched her tighter against him. He tugged at her lips, sucking the bottom one into his mouth. He wanted more. She tasted like the firelight and moonshine, sweet, smoky and hot enough to burn. And yet, there was an innocence lurking just beneath the surface as well.

His tongue swept inside, exploring, invading, taking. He caressed her, teasing and soothing, drawing them both closer to the point of frenzy.

He wanted to go slow, to give her an experience she wouldn't forget. But with that first taste he knew he didn't have the willpower. Not after fighting his desire for the past two days.

Her mouth was soft and pliant. Knox drank in every whimper, sigh and groan like the prizes they all were.

Avery's fingers gripped him, silently compelling him to keep going.

But he didn't. Instead, he pulled away.

He had to find some sanity or they were both going to have regrets. And that was the last thing he wanted.

Knox had enough of those in his life.

Avery's judgment was impaired. He knew she wouldn't have asked him if she'd been sober...or if they'd been on the *Amphitrite* instead of a deserted island. Which, incidentally, was his fault as well.

So, like any good soldier, he surveyed the landscape and formulated a plan of attack that would satisfy both her need and his conscience.

If he could hold his shit together.

Digging down deep, Knox searched for the discipline the Navy had taught him. He was going to need it.

Avery stared up at him, her pale blue eyes no longer cool, but a raging inferno of need. She was panting as if she'd just run a 5K.

He could read her nervous uncertainty, liked her that much more for the glimpse of vulnerability. "Every girl's dream. To be cursed at then kissed," she said on a tiny laugh.

It took him a second to figure out what she meant.

"I wasn't cursing at you, Avery. I was cursing myself for not having the strength to say no to you.

Shifting, Knox reached for the shirt he'd left on the sand and rolled it into a tube. Lifting her head, he replaced his thigh with the shirt and then stretched out beside her.

Smoothing his hands down her body, Knox stared into her eyes, looking for any sign that she wasn't as certain as she seemed.

"You're sure this is what you want?"

She swallowed, the elegant line of her throat working

even as she nodded. All he could see was crystal-clear need, the same thing that was pulsing through his own body.

At least one of them should find some relief.

With deft fingers, Knox pulled the hem of her shirt up over her head and tossed it somewhere on the sand behind him. Underneath she was wearing a pale blue bra covered in beige lace. It was sweet yet sexy, not unlike, he was coming to realize, the woman who owned it.

"Please tell me your panties match this," he murmured against her mouth, trailing a single finger over the strap at her shoulder.

She shivered at the gentle caress, arching into his touch in a way that told him she wanted more.

"Maybe you should find out," she whispered, grasping his hand and drawing it down to the zipper on her shorts.

Tugging at the tab, he slowly pulled it down, but kept his gaze focused squarely on Avery's eyes. He couldn't look away, not even to see what he was revealing.

Because her expression exposed more.

The way her pupils dilated, pushing against the pale blue in the same way he wanted to push deep into her body. The heat and hesitation—not because she wasn't sure about what they were doing, but because she was as overwhelmed as he was.

He was afraid that once this line was crossed, they'd never be able to go back. But he was doing it anyway. Couldn't stop himself, not when Avery's lips were parted slightly, air rushing in and out of her moist mouth.

She swayed into his touch and that was all the reassurance he needed.

She didn't wait for him to push the shorts off, but lifted her hips and did the job herself, revealing panties that absolutely matched, although they were more lace than anything else. And the glimpses of skin through the tiny holes only made him want to see more.

He hadn't expected anything less. The rest of her wardrobe was too precise for what went under it to be haphazard.

Not that he minded. And knowing what she hid beneath those damn business clothes was going to drive him insane the next time she put them on.

Arching her spine off the sand, she reached behind her back and popped the catch of her bra.

"Am I not moving fast enough for you?"

"No." She shook her head. "These clothes are too tight. It feels like I'm suffocating. My skin is on fire."

Was that him or the moonshine? Or the heat from the flames beside them?

Not that it mattered.

A part of him wanted to undress her, but he couldn't deny himself the privilege of watching her uncover her body. For him.

Hooking fingers into her panties, Avery pushed until they slid to her ankles before kicking them off.

Completely naked, with the firelight flickering across her skin, she was absolutely breathtaking. The most gorgeous woman he'd ever seen.

And she'd revealed something intriguing.

Dropping to the sand between her thighs, Knox placed his palms on her bent knees and pressed outward. Even as her thighs fell open, he leaned down to study her left hip.

The last thing he'd expected to find was a tattoo. Avery didn't strike him as the kind of woman to want to permanently mark her skin.

But the ink was as intricately beautiful as it was unanticipated. An eye in perfectly shaded black and white, dripping tears of brilliant orange, red and gold koi fish.

Knox traced the lines with the roughened pad of his finger. He wanted to ask her about it, but now wasn't the time.

Poised between her open thighs, Knox glanced up to find her watching him. The cloudy, dreamy expression that had entered her gaze a few swallows into the alcohol was gone, replaced by a wariness that nearly stole his breath.

She was waiting for him to say…what?

For the first time, Knox realized the languid easiness that had invaded her muscles was gone. She'd pressed her legs tight against his sides, closing herself off as much as his hips and shoulders would let her.

In that brief moment, he thought about stopping, but the vulnerability in her eyes wouldn't let him. Not even as his brain screamed it was the smart thing to do.

Allowing his finger to caress the lines of her ink, he said, "Beautiful."

And the tension that had invaded her body leaked back out again.

Leaning up, Avery reached for him, going for the waistband of his shorts and trying to get them undone.

But there was no way he could handle that right now. Not and keep his sanity.

Wrapping his fingers around her wrists, Knox stalled her. "No."

She stilled. "What do you mean, no?"

He didn't really give her an answer, partly because he didn't think she'd like it, but mostly because he didn't want to take the chance that she'd argue with him. He was fighting himself as it was; he didn't think he could handle fighting her on this as well.

Pressing against her knees, Knox urged her to open wide. His palm skated down the inside of her upper thigh, delighting in the delicate, soft feel of her against his palms.

He followed that with his lips, pressing openmouthed

kisses from the bend of her knee all the way up to the crease at her hip and back down the other side. He wasn't certain when she dropped back onto the sand, not that it mattered.

Not when each tiny whimper that fell through her parted lips echoed through his chest. Not when her hips squirmed and arched, silently begging for more. Not when the scent of her arousal filled his nostrils, driving out every thought except how she would taste.

He was almost as desperate for it as she was by the time he let his tongue slide across the wet slit of her sex.

"God, you taste so damn good," he managed to groan out, even as he went in for more.

His hands spread wide across her hips, holding her captive.

He could stay between her thighs all night, drinking in her little moans as he lapped up every drop of her arousal.

Knox worked her over, taking his time and enjoying the way her body tightened, drawing closer and closer to an explosion he wanted for them both.

She arched up each time he dipped his tongue inside her opening. He loved her little sounds and the way the tiny bundle of nerves at the top hardened with each passing lick or deliberate press of his tongue.

Sucking it into his mouth, he relished her whimper when he gently placed the edges of his teeth on either side and stopped, letting anticipation, adrenaline and the moist heat of his mouth drive her crazy.

There was something so satisfying about knowing he had the power to make her mindless with need. Knowing he alone could break through that perfect facade and see her like this, flushed with passion and longing. It was a beautiful gift, one he had every intention of earning.

"Knox, please," she begged, her fingers tugging hard at

his hair even as she writhed beneath the weight of him pinning her down, searching for relief. "Please, I can't take…"

"Shh, I've got you, doc," he murmured against her.

Slipping two fingers inside, he delighted in the way she bucked against his hand. Curling his fingers, he found that magic spot deep inside and began to stroke in steady, even thrusts.

His own erection ached in time with the pulses fluttering through her body. He could feel it, pounding so hard he was afraid he might explode before he had the chance to make her come.

And, damn, he wanted to see that. Wanted to see her completely unravel. Hold her through that storm and be the first thing she saw on the other side.

Knox flicked his tongue across her clit in time with the thrust of his fingers. It was an orchestrated rhythm that had her bowing up and her mouth opening on a silent scream.

Her orgasm hit them both. Knox had to fight back the urge to pump against the soft curve of her hip and find his own relief, he was so damn close. The way her sex clenched and released, holding his fingers hostage made him desperate to drop his shorts and push inside.

But that wasn't going to happen.

Knox coaxed her through the orgasm, drawing out the pleasure, not just for her, but because he was greedy and wanted every last whimper he could wring from her.

When her body quieted, collapsing bonelessly beneath him, Knox crawled up to lie on the sand beside her.

Wrapping his arms around her body, he pulled her back against him.

They were both breathing hard. He could feel the knock of her heart against the band of his arm where it stretched across her chest.

He should probably find her clothes, cover her up. It would likely get a little chilly in the middle of the night, even if they were in the Caribbean.

But he didn't have the energy or the willpower to let her go right now.

For some strange reason, the thought of not touching her sent panic fluttering through his belly.

Slowly, her breathing evened and her heartbeat returned to normal. She stirred in his arms. At first, he tightened his hold, thinking she was trying to put distance between them. And he wasn't ready to let her do that.

But when he realized she just wanted to reposition herself, he let her go.

She rolled, turning so that they were face-to-face with the fire at her back.

She glanced up at him and then back down. "You didn't…"

Knox tangled his fingers in her hair, bending her back so he could look her in the eye. "No. That was for you."

"Oh."

Her body stiffened. Tucked so tightly against his, it was a cue that was damn near impossible to miss.

Little white teeth dug into her bottom lip, but the move couldn't completely hide the pull of a frown. Nodding, she slipped away, and this time he let her go.

Standing up, she prowled through the dark. Knox rolled onto his back to watch her slip her clothes back on beneath the cover of the shadows.

Somehow it felt like a metaphor for whatever had just happened.

He was confused by her reaction. He'd just given her a damn good orgasm and denied himself one too because he didn't want to take advantage of her when her judgment was impaired.

Vaulting to his feet, Knox moved after her. Grasping her arm, he urged her around to face him.

"What's wrong, Avery?" His voice was slow and deliberate. Maybe a little tighter than he'd meant, but that was probably because his dick was so damn hard he was fairly sure that any second it was going to punch through the steel zipper holding his shorts closed.

"Nothing."

Oh, no, she didn't.

Burying his hand in the hair at her nape, Knox pulled her up on her toes and fused his mouth with hers. It was the best way he knew to bleed off some of the tension before he exploded.

He was panting and she was glaring when he pulled back seconds later. But she'd responded to him, opening her mouth and tangling her tongue with his when he invaded.

"We both know that's a lie, doc. Want to try that again?"

"I just…" Her gaze slipped away from him. And her body sagged in his hold. He drew her closer, sharing his strength.

"I'm not used to this kind of thing. Sex for the sake of sex. I've only had three lovers. And, frankly, none of them ever came close to making me feel what you just did. It…" She finally looked back at him, her expression filled with confusion. "…bothers me that you didn't take anything. I feel like I owe you now. I wasn't looking for a pity orgasm."

Jesus, this woman was going to be the death of him. How could she be so worldly and sophisticated one minute and shockingly naive the next?

The problem was, he liked that about her. Liked that she could surprise him.

Not many people did.

One of his greatest skills was reading people. It had come in handy on plenty of missions, as guys turned to him to evaluate whether to trust an informant or interrogate captives.

He couldn't quite read Avery. Well, not reliably, anyway. It was refreshing and maddening all at once.

"What about what just happened made you think that was pity, Avery?"

Taking her hand, he cupped it around his erection and hissed a breath through his teeth at the contact. "What about this makes you think I don't want you?"

Her grip tightened, sending all the blood in his body rushing to his groin. In a minute, he wouldn't have enough left for his brain to function. Wrapping his fingers around her wrist, he pulled her away. The move was torture and self-preservation rolled into one.

"But—"

Knox cut her off before her softly spoken words were his complete undoing. Honor was important to him. Always had been, but the SEALs had pounded the ideal into his head so deep it was embedded in his skull. He wouldn't be able to forgive himself if he did what he knew Avery was about to suggest.

When she was sober. When they were back in civilization and not stranded together on an island with the threat of never being found looming over their heads, even if the emergency beacon made that possibility remote. Then, if she still wanted him in her bed, he would gladly take her up on the offer.

Until then...

"It's late. We both need sleep."

Scooping her up, Knox walked back to the fire. Gently, he set her on the ground and then followed her down. Placing her close to the fire, he wrapped an arm around her waist and pulled her tight against his body, tucking her head beneath his chin and positioning her with his biceps as a pillow.

Her body was stiff. His hand settled on her tummy, and he was a little grateful she'd put her clothes back on. He needed all the barriers he could get.

Bending, he buried his nose in her hair and breathed in the clean fragrance of her shampoo, some herbs he didn't know the names of.

She pulled in a deep breath, held it for several seconds, and then let it free, all the tension leaving her body with it.

And then all the tension left his, well, everything except the residual arousal he wasn't going to shake as long as Avery was in his arms. But he'd live with that.

He thought she was already asleep, her breathing slow and even, when her soft words drifted over him.

"Seriously, Knox, best orgasm of my life. Thanks."

He chuckled. "You're welcome."

The woman was a constant surprise.

# 7

AVERY SQUINTED. EVEN THROUGH her closed lids, the glare of sunlight made her head ache. No, wait, made everything ache. Her entire body throbbed with a steady, dull thump—a combination of alcohol, sleeping on the ground and amazing sex.

Knox McLemore had given her the best orgasm of her life. He'd played her body better than men she'd dated for months.

And he hadn't taken a thing for himself. That bothered her, and she didn't know what to do with it. Which only bothered her more. She wanted to regret last night. Knew she should probably feel embarrassed and guilty, but she didn't.

Although, heat did sweep up her skin at the memory of how wanton and uninhibited she'd been. Damn moonshine.

It was probably a good thing she'd woken up by herself instead of still tucked against Knox's hard body. His biceps might be works of art, but all those muscles were hard to sleep on.

Rolling onto her back, Avery draped her arm over her

face to shield herself from the glare of the sun already high above.

She couldn't remember the last time she'd slept this late. Although not having an alarm, or any place to be, helped. It was actually…nice, although she'd be loath to admit that to anyone.

Actually, now that she thought about it, the warm sun on her skin felt good. A decadent indulgence. Without thinking, she arched her back, stretching tight muscles.

"Now that's a welcome sight to walk up on."

The low rumble of Knox's voice melted down her spine. Her body reacted, a warm buzz slipping just beneath her skin. She found him standing in the cool shadows of the tree line.

He moved forward out of the shade, the shorts he'd worn yesterday slung low on his hips.

Knox watched her with that lazy, calculating gaze. It was an act, a shield, and she was beginning to realize he saw much more than she'd originally given him credit for.

She wondered why he hid behind it, but didn't think it was appropriate to ask. Mostly because she wanted the answer more than she should.

But beneath that stare, her body responded, memories of last night rushing to the surface. A blush heated her skin. At this point embarrassment seemed silly, and yet she couldn't stop it. Not when he was gauging her every response.

Propped against a tree several yards away, he cocked his head. His mouth tilted up on one side. "How are you this morning, doc?"

"Sore."

He nodded. "I'd offer you moonshine, but I emptied the bottle and filled it with water."

For the first time, Avery realized the bottle from last

night was wedged into the ground at the edge of the fire pit, the water inside the clear glass lazily bubbling from the residual heat.

"You've been busy this morning."

He shrugged, slowly pushing against the tree and strolling in her direction. "Couldn't sleep."

She immediately felt like a jerk. While she'd been luxuriating in no alarm clock, he'd been seeing to their survival and basic needs.

"I'm sorry," she said, rolling to her knees and pushing to her feet. Sand ground uncomfortably against her skin, but that was something she could remedy later. The bright side was that they had plenty of water to wash off in.

Knox didn't stop until his hands cupped her upper arms, his thumbs rubbing gentle circles on her warm skin. She could feel the space between them, small yet somehow cavernous.

She glanced down. His toes dug into the sand, flexing. She'd never particularly paid attention to a man's toes before. But she liked his.

What the hell was wrong with her?

An unwanted burn crept up her neck. Her involuntary reaction frustrated her. Left her feeling less than in control of an already slippery situation.

"I don't mind, Avery."

"Maybe not, but I do. I should have helped."

His mouth twitched. "Well, why don't you help with breakfast, then?"

He gestured to a spit where a hunk of meat that looked suspiciously rodent shaped was suspended over the glowing coals.

"What is it?"

"I have no idea, but I'm hoping it tastes like rabbit."

Avery's eyes went wide. "You've eaten rabbit?"

He chuckled, his hands slipping down her arms and then back up over her shoulders to tangle his fingers in her hair. It was probably a complete wreck, all snarls and knots.

"I've eaten all sorts of things you probably don't want to know about. Rabbit is possibly the least offensive."

Avery's mouth twisted into an unhappy line as her gaze moved back to the sizzling meat.

"I managed to catch it while I was getting water. I was planning on spearfishing later, but there's no reason to ignore fresh meat now."

If it didn't still have a face she might be more inclined to eat it without shuddering.

But he'd caught it for them, prepared it and cooked it. Growing up, the rule had been that unless you wanted chef duty next, you didn't complain. And considering she didn't have the skills necessary to feed them, she wasn't going to say a word.

"Thanks." She shifted on her feet, glancing up at him and then away.

Avery was used to being in command, of herself and the circumstances around her. There was nothing about this that felt in her control. In fact, from the moment she'd heard the name Trident Diving and Salvage, her life had been in complete chaos.

McNair was threatening her and pushing her to do something she'd regret for the rest of her life. But she was afraid she didn't have much choice. With her parents refusing to be in her sister's life even after the accident, Melody depended on her. Without the money her business brought in, they wouldn't be able to afford the care facility where she lived.

Since Avery had moved her there six years ago, Melody had been making strides in her recovery. She'd regained some speech and motor skills. Taking her out of that environment was unthinkable.

She'd do whatever she had to in order to ensure her sister's care remained constant.

Then there was Knox. With his fingers tangled in her hair and his body so close she could feel his heat soaking into her skin, she just wanted to lean into him and accept the strength and comfort he probably didn't even realize she needed.

And then she wanted him to make her scream again.

But that couldn't happen.

Last night her judgment had been clouded. This morning it was clear.

No matter what happened, Knox was going to be angry with her, thanks to McNair.

Apparently, he'd been right not to completely give in last night. Although she couldn't quite muster up the energy to regret what had happened.

"Don't do that," he said, his voice soft even as his thumb smoothed over the ridges crinkled between her eyebrows.

"Don't do what?"

"Don't second-guess what happened."

"How did you…" Avery shook her head. "I'm not second-guessing, not really. I'm…upset that you were right to hold back and disappointed it can't happen again."

"Mmm," Knox murmured, the single sound somehow managing to convey that he understood and shared her disappointment.

Using his leverage, he drew her closer, up onto her tiptoes. Her heart lurched and her breath stalled inside her chest. She could have moved, could have pulled away from him. But she didn't.

With the pressure of his thumb underneath her chin, he

tipped her head back and ran the pad down her exposed throat. An unwanted shiver rocked her body.

His steady gaze caught her, held her prisoner just as surely as his hands in her hair. This morning there wasn't the same blaze of unbelievable heat that had consumed them both the night before. But there was something else. Still a burn, but more gentle.

Something had changed last night. A tiny voice inside her head whispered, *You're in too deep now, girl.*

Slowly, Knox lowered his lips to hers, brushing them softly together. Her brain screamed at her to hold still, not react. But her body didn't cooperate. Her lips parted, inviting him in.

The kiss was warm and silky. Comforting and effortless. It was like melted chocolate and sunshine.

Avery heard herself sigh, the breathy kind of sound she'd often condemned other women for making, calling them stupid for letting their baser urges rule them. But that was because she hadn't understood. Had never experienced the overwhelming sensation of wanting someone so much it trumped everything.

Her body relaxed, going languid. Her hands found his shoulders and slipped down across the hair-roughened skin of his chest.

After several moments, Knox pulled back. His lips were moist. Avery supposed hers were as well. She wanted more, but there was something in the way he was looking at her that kept her still.

"Good morning," he murmured.

Avery struggled to find her voice. "Uh, hi," she finally said.

"You better be careful or you're going to get burned." Knox let a single fingertip trail across from collarbone to collarbone where her shirt left the top of her chest exposed.

She hated her skin, pale and freckled, but it came with her bright red hair. Although, she'd never been particularly enamored of that either.

Being a redhead meant she usually stuck out in a crowd. Especially when she was younger and they'd lived in places where red hair was even more unusual. Maybe all the times when she was little and heard women chattering in a language she didn't understand, their eyes cutting to her so it was obvious they were talking about her, had bred her dislike for being the center of attention.

Or maybe that inclination was just naturally her.

Those experiences had definitely fueled her drive, as she'd gotten older, to learn the language whenever they'd moved on to someplace new.

Either way, she'd never particularly liked the notice her hair drew. And it had only gotten worse as she'd grown older, started to develop.

The icing on the cake had been the night her entire world had fallen apart.

Melody had been running with a bad crowd while their father had been on a dig just off the coast of Spain, near Morocco. She'd gotten tired of the constant arguments between her parents and her sister. Her sister willfully broke every rule she could, seemingly for spite.

She hadn't liked the friends Melody brought by the house. They were rough, rude and delighted in making her feel uncomfortable. On several occasions the guys had made inappropriate comments to her when she'd inadvertently walked into the kitchen or the den and found them sprawled there.

Even she had become angry with Melody for her lack of respect. The house was Avery's sanctuary and it hurt that she couldn't walk around her own home without the fear of being heckled and propositioned.

But the straw that broke the camel's back had been the night she'd woken up in her own room with one of Melody's friends standing over her bed. At first, she'd thought the guy was looking for Melody. Until he'd said her name, his voice slurred.

"So gorgeous, *canela*," he'd said in his thickly accented voice as his fingers sifted through her hair. Cinnamon. She hated the way he'd said the word, because it wasn't an endearment but somehow a threat. His other hand rested heavily on her hip, pinning her against the bed when she tried to move away.

She'd gone still, hoping all he wanted was to scare her. But that wasn't what he wanted. The bed had dipped beneath his weight. His hand had gripped her hair, pulling hard until tears stung her eyes.

"I wonder if that color is natural. Your sister says yes. I must know for myself." His other hand slipped beneath the waistband of her shorts, yanking.

It had taken her several moments to react, but when the shock wore off a sharp scream burst out. His hand slapped down over her mouth, but it had been enough.

Her father had come running. Beat the shit out of guy before tossing him into the street. That night, the arguments had been bad. Melody, angry and belligerent, claiming she'd overreacted. Fed up, her parents had kicked Melody out, offering her a plane ticket home that she hadn't used.

Four weeks later they'd moved home to Texas, back into the house her parents owned but had barely used over the years. Avery had begun applying for early entrance to colleges. Everyone pretended that their family hadn't been broken by what happened, but the facade had shattered six months later when they'd gotten the call saying that Melody had been arrested for drug possession.

"I'll be careful not to burn," Avery finally said, choking off the unwanted memories.

Knox tipped his head, his gaze roaming across her expression. Once again, Avery sensed that he saw much more than she wanted him to. But instead of asking what had caused the strange catch in her voice, he took a step back, waving toward the fire.

Together they sat down to the meal he'd prepared. It wasn't the first time she'd eaten a questionable protein source around a fire. On some of her father's more exotic digs, they'd been invited to partake in local delicacies.

The meat was tough but decent, the smokiness from being roasted over the fire providing enough flavor for her to choke it down. Knox watched her, a smirk playing at the corners of his mouth as she picked at the bones.

"Nautical archaeology. That's a pretty narrow field. How'd you end up there?" he asked, filling the silence. Things between them had become considerably more comfortable since last night. She supposed they'd released some sexual tension…well, at least she had.

It was Avery's turn to study him. "Why do you want to know?"

"Call it curiosity."

Was it possible he was feeling as off-kilter as she was, searching for solid ground, or was he trying to expose her true purpose?

Either way, she didn't see the harm in answering. Maybe they could end up friends, at least until she betrayed him and royally screwed his business.

"I started out in anthropology. I've always been fascinated with people, cultures. My father is an archaeologist and most of my playgrounds contained ancient artifacts and dig quadrants instead of monkey bars and swing sets."

"Well, that explains a lot."

"What's that supposed to mean?"

Knox shook his head. "Down, killer. I just meant that you have an air about you. A sophistication that goes beyond the pearls and heels. It's experience. Seeing the world, people and different cultures, and learning to appreciate the value they bring."

"You understand."

Knox tossed a bone into the fire. The flames flared and sizzled. "Admittedly, I've seen a different side of the world than you probably have."

"I wouldn't count on that," Avery mumbled under her breath, the unhappy memories too close to the surface not to be in the forefront of her mind.

Knox gave her a questioning glance, but didn't comment.

"The effect is the same. Sometimes our lives can feel so small, our problems so huge, until we're faced with desperate mothers, fathers broken because they can't provide for their families, and children forced to take on responsibilities at eight or nine that no child should."

Avery nodded. He did understand.

No, she hadn't spent years of her life in war-torn countries as Knox had, but she'd seen enough poverty, starvation and oppression in the countries she had visited. It was always difficult for her to witness those things. As a teenager she'd felt powerless to do anything to help.

"Although—" his tawny eyes glinted with mischief "—I will say that for someone interested in learning about people, you really have no idea how to interact with them."

Pulling her hand back, Avery aimed her own bone at Knox's head. He didn't even flinch, simply snatched it out of the air before it got anywhere close to him, cocked a single eyebrow at her and redirected it into the fire.

"Nice aim, doc."

"Show-off," she grumbled, although there wasn't much heat behind the word. "Those who can't do, teach. Those who can't interact, study human civilizations in an attempt to understand others."

"And pay the bills."

Avery couldn't stop the smile from tugging at her lips. "And pay the bills."

Avery shifted, crossing her legs in front of her and grabbing a handful of sand. The grains fell through her fingers, silky and sugary fine.

"Believe it or not, I'm better than I used to be." She studied him from beneath her lashes. "You seem to draw out the worst in me."

A grin flashed across his face—almost before it was there it was gone—leaving behind a banked heat.

"I seem to remember bringing out the best in you last night." Warmth climbed through her, pooling right between her thighs. Her breasts felt heavy and swollen and she wished she'd bothered to find her bra last night before tossing her tank back on, but it had been nearly impossible in the dark. Now, she knew the thin material would provide no barrier to the sharp points of her nipples.

"At least, that's what you said right before you fell asleep."

The grin he tossed her was impish and a little wicked. A combination of irritation and arousal rioted through her body. Knox seemed to know just what buttons to push... and exactly when to push them.

"Wanker."

"British swearwords? Doc, your ice princess is showing again."

She wanted to laugh, but wouldn't let herself. Mostly

because he was only half-joking. "Has anyone ever told you you're a cocky asshole, Knox McLemore?"

"On several occasions, but thanks for playing. We have some nice parting gifts."

"That wasn't a compliment."

His face sobered. Avery wasn't certain when the good-natured ribbing—something they seemed to delight in as a sort of foreplay—morphed into something more real. "I realize you didn't mean it as one. But I promise there are worse things to be called."

"Such as…"

Smoke billowed between them, obscuring the outline of his body for several seconds. It undulated, a frosted veil she couldn't see clearly through. From behind the smoke a single word drifted up. "Murderer."

The way he said it…it wasn't a word he'd pulled out of the air, like *terrorist*. Now that, given his background, would have made more sense.

No, he said it with sadness and ownership that she didn't understand.

"I'm guessing most murderers wouldn't particularly care about carrying the label."

The smoke drifting between them cleared.

"You'd be wrong."

Her eyes locked with his. There was something in the way he looked at her—challenge, maybe. He was daring her to voice the obvious question.

Which was why she didn't.

She didn't understand what was behind his statement, but she knew Knox well enough—despite their short time together—to realize that while he obviously believed what he'd said, it wasn't true. It couldn't be.

The man who'd refused to accept what she was offering last night, because it went against some internal code about taking advantage, wouldn't hurt anyone. Not without justification.

That much she recognized about Knox McLemore. And right now, that was more than enough.

## 8

WHERE THE HELL was Asher? Frustration mixed with a tiny trickle of fear sat heavily across Knox's shoulders.

Avery stood at the edge of the beach, staring out across the open water. The sun was beginning its descent to the far horizon. He'd really hoped they'd be rescued by now.

As much as he tried to focus on other things—which had been easy when they'd needed water, food and shelter—now that the basics were covered, his mind kept circling back to one indisputable fact.

Their predicament was entirely his fault. If he hadn't rushed after that box like a reckless cowboy, Avery wouldn't be in this mess.

They could be stuck out here for weeks. Months. He knew Jackson, Asher, Kennedy and Loralei wouldn't stop looking for them, but eventually the beacon would die and their one link to the outside world would disappear.

He'd been in worse scrapes…he just hadn't dragged a civilian into them with him—although, he had to admit, Avery was handling things much better than he'd expected.

But he didn't like being powerless, and while there was plenty to keep him physically occupied—building them shelter, fishing, exploring their island—there was nothing more he could do to improve their odds of being rescued.

He longed for something to quiet his brain and the self-recriminations that were less than helpful. Although, when he wasn't thinking about that, his mind kept circling back to sex with Avery. And while that idea had kept his cock half-hard the entire day, that wasn't how he wanted her—as a distraction. Because she was much more than that.

And without the swirl of darkness and moonshine, he was too aware that he didn't actually trust Avery, even if he was beginning to really like her.

The need humming just beneath the surface of his skin didn't really help. In fact, it made the whole damn situation worse.

He had to find another outlet. Fast. What he wouldn't give for a punching bag and gloves…or Asher's face. Either would work.

Well, there was one way to exhaust his body. Stripping down to his boxer briefs, Knox didn't bother looking behind him as he waded out into the water and dived beneath the surface.

Unlike Jackson, he hadn't grown up diving, although he had been a competitive swimmer. In fact, he hadn't discovered his love for scuba diving until he joined the Navy. And then it had become more of a personal crusade. He'd needed the skill in order to be successful with the SEALs.

Jackson had once described the sense of calm and peace he found beneath the waves. Knox had envied him that. Wanted desperately to find it for himself. He liked diving. Enjoyed watching the beautiful creatures that called the oceans home. But the water had become more of an office for him than an escape.

Now, the open road…that was where he felt free. A perfect fall morning, winding country roads and absolutely no destination in mind as he pushed the needle on his Shelby well past the speed limit.

He imagined that's where he was, the water flowing across his body becoming the kiss of the wind. He had no idea how long he spent swimming the perimeter of the cove, not that it really mattered. By the time he headed for shore, exhaustion dragged at his muscles. Good, that was exactly what he needed.

Or that's what he thought until he started back toward their makeshift camp.

He froze, that delicious exhaustion disappearing in a single, debilitating blast of awareness.

"What are you doing?"

Avery had folded herself into a triangle. Her round rear, covered by her shorts, was high in the air and pointed straight in his direction. It didn't take any time at all for his libido to kick in and suggest the perfect use for that position.

As he watched, she transitioned, dropping to the ground and folding her legs one over the other before twisting her shoulders sideways. The move looked complicated and painful, but didn't appear to be bothering her at all. She kept her gaze focused ahead of her, ignoring him completely.

Knox stepped closer, kicking up tiny bursts of sand, but careful not to send them in her direction. "What are you doing?"

Avery breathed deeply, her chest expanding. He couldn't look away from the up-and-down motion of her breasts.

"Yoga."

"That's not what I meant. *Why* are you doing yoga?"

"You should try it."

She moved, her body fluid and graceful.

"No, thanks."

Bent into a pretzel, she stared up at him from between her legs with that superior expression that drove him nuts. He hadn't seen it for a while. Wondered what it would take to make it disappear again.

"Afraid?"

"Doc, I'm afraid of two things, bombs and men with nothing to live for."

She sucked in a sharp breath and Knox immediately regretted the delivery, if not the actual statement.

Grinding out a curse word beneath his breath, Knox plopped onto the sand beside her.

He reached for her ankle and gently tugged until she unwound from her pretzel position.

"I'm sorry."

"For what?"

"Being an asshole."

Avery laughed, the sound a little harsh. "Accepted. Want to tell me what crawled up your ass and died?"

Knox sighed, dropped onto his back in the sand and pillowed his arms behind his neck. He twisted his head so that he could look up at her.

The sun was a burst of fire behind her head, gilding her hair with coppery highlights. She watched him, patiently waiting. That was something he valued about Avery, a gift her quiet, contained nature gave him when he didn't even realize he needed it. No pressure, just acceptance.

"I'm worried."

"That Asher hasn't shown up yet?"

He nodded.

"So am I, but I'm sure he'll find us eventually."

Knox let out a sigh and closed his eyes. It was the *eventually* that bothered him most. "I'm sorry."

"You already said that."

"For getting you into this. I shouldn't have raced after that box. It was stupid and reckless."

He peeked over at her through the glaring sun, expecting to find her frowning, but instead she wore one of her rare and brilliant smiles.

"Why are you smiling at me?"

"Because I didn't expect you to ever admit that was a boneheaded idea, Mr. I Have a Plan. Thanks, by the way, but it isn't necessary. I was just as curious."

"Curious maybe, but you wouldn't have done something so stupid."

"Oh, I wouldn't count on that either. I've done plenty of boneheaded things in my life. When I was fifteen, there was this dig in South America, an ancient temple they'd found deep in the jungle. I wanted to go, but my parents wouldn't let me. I was stuck back at the village while my dad had all the fun. So, one morning I snuck onto a supply truck and rode out there. Little did I know the dig site was right in the middle of a guerilla terrorist group's territory. I was grounded for a month when my parents discovered what I'd done."

"Poor little Avery," Knox drawled.

She reached out and shoved him, but before she could pull back, Knox snagged her wrists, holding her bent over him. He stared up into her gaze, reveling in the flare of heat that blasted through her ice-blue eyes.

She wasn't drunk. He wasn't either. He still wanted her, and if the peaks of her nipples and her stuttering breath were any indication, she wanted him as well.

Knox was tired of fighting.

Drawing her down to him, he claimed her mouth. There was nothing slow or seductive about the kiss. He'd lost that kind of finesse hours ago. Now he just needed her, with a desperation that crackled beneath his skin.

But she didn't seem to mind. In fact, Avery pressed closer, throwing one leg over his hip so that her sex lined up perfectly with the throbbing ridge of his erection.

She moaned, the sound sending a burning shot of need straight through him.

"Avery," he groaned. Sitting up, he wrapped his arms around her body, pressing her down tight against his cock caught between them. Pure torture and unbelievable pleasure. Especially when she started moving, her hips undulating against him.

He had to touch her. Taste her. "I need you. Right now."

His hands ripped at her clothes, finesse out the window. Eventually he managed to drag her tank top over her head, all the while latching his lips to any patch of skin he could find.

She tasted like heaven, sweet and salty and perfectly Avery. The scent of her overwhelmed him, vanilla and clear blue sky.

Her hands scrambled over his body, just as eager as he was. She ran the soft pads of her fingers up and down his chest, abs, ribs. Wherever she touched, the lick of lightning followed, electrifying him like nothing else in his life had ever done.

He was in trouble. No question about it. But he no longer cared.

Bending down, he sucked a tight nipple into his mouth. Another groan erupted from his throat, vibrating between them both. Avery's breath caught. She was pressed so tightly against him, he could feel the stutter of it.

"Knox," she sighed, the sound complete surrender as she arched back, offering him more.

Knox wanted everything.

He was tugging at her zipper, ready to break the thing to get to her moist heat, when a sound stopped him.

"Knox?" She said again, pulling back.

As much as he didn't want to, Knox stilled beneath her. The sound was out of place, enough that instinct kicked in and his entire system went on alert, adrenaline that had nothing to do with desire pumping into his system.

After a few more seconds of listening, Knox wrapped his hands around Avery's hips, lifting her off and setting her softly back onto the ground.

She blinked up at him, bewildered, eyes still glazed with desire.

Shielding his face from the setting sun, Knox looked out and saw the small motorboat approaching.

In seconds Asher was pulling up into the cove.

"You have the worst timing, my friend!" Knox shouted across the water.

"Would you like me to leave and come back later?" Asher hollered back.

Jumping to her feet, Avery screamed, "Not on your life," even as she yanked her tank back on.

"What took you so long?" Knox groused, glaring at Asher as his friend stepped free of the launch and onto the sand.

Asher simply grinned. "I see a night out under the stars did wonders for your disposition." He walked right past Knox, pretty much ignoring him as he cut straight for Avery.

"It took us a while to realize you guys were gone…and in trouble. And then to catch the signal from the locating beacon. Imagine my surprise to find it on a tiny island not listed on any map," Asher tossed over his shoulder.

Asher scooped Avery up in a huge bear hug. Her arms and legs dangled as he twisted her back and forth. "Good to see you."

Avery stared at Knox over Asher's shoulder, not quite able to suppress the tinge of pink that touched her cheeks.

"Put her down, you idiot," Knox growled, a combination of warning and amusement shading his voice.

Turning away, Knox snagged the clothes he'd left on the shore before going for his swim and tugged the shorts and shirt back on.

"You all right, doc?" Asher asked, dropping her back down to the sand.

Asher might have the reputation as a ladies' man, but that was because he truly had an appreciation for all females. Short, tall, athletic, curvy, old, young, it didn't matter. He was just as gentle and attentive with the grandmother who needed help carrying her groceries as he was with the bombshells who sent him drinks at the bar.

It shouldn't bother Knox, the way his friend moved in on Avery, pushing close and invading her personal space. He shouldn't want to rip Asher's hand away from where it rested against her arm. But he did.

Knox fought against the unwanted possessive reaction. Women were the one thing he and his friends had never fought over. And he wasn't about to let that change today.

Besides, he wasn't the jealous type. Or had never been before.

"I'm fine," he heard Avery say.

"I have to admit, doc, you look a little worse for wear."

He had the urge to defend her, but he should have curbed the reaction because Avery was perfectly capable of taking care of herself. "You try sleeping on the sand and see how fresh you look, sunshine."

"Don't get me wrong, you're still gorgeous, just a little rumpled." Asher grinned. "Pretty sure I like you better rumpled, Firecracker."

Knox let out a low growl that startled even him.

Avery shifted, shooting him a cautioning glare. Jesus, he needed to get hold of himself.

"Leave her alone. She's had an exhausting couple of days and isn't up to dealing with you at full wattage."

Asher shrugged.

His friend shifted and for the first time Knox registered the tension pulling his shoulders straight. He should have known, and if he'd been thinking about anything other than his interrupted interlude with Avery, he would have.

Asher's charm was more often than not an act he used to hide everything else bubbling beneath the surface. His friend had been genuinely concerned, as would he have been if their roles were reversed.

Crossing the sand, Asher clapped him on the back and Knox returned the gesture. They'd been through a lot over the years and had the scars to prove it.

"You wanna tell me what the hell happened? Where's our boat?"

Knox sighed, exhaustion pulling at him now that he knew everything was going to be okay.

"We both need a shower, food and sleep."

"All of that is already waiting. I'm certain Catherine is working on the fatted calf as we speak, but you're going to have to share with the class before I let you sleep, man."

Knox nodded. "Let me get her settled first."

Walking over to Avery, he didn't bother asking before scooping her up into his arms. She let out a protest, but wrapped her hands tight around his neck.

"Knox, put me down."

Asher's eyebrows rose. His gaze drilled into Knox's for several seconds. And then a wide, knowing grin spread across his face.

"Nope."

"Asher, make him put me down," she growled.

His friend was no fool. Hands drifting upward in the "I

surrender" sign, he backed away. "Sorry, Firecracker, no can do."

She let out a disgruntled huff. "This is stupid. I can walk."

"I'm sure you can, but I'm not idiot enough to get in Knox's path when he's made up his mind to be chivalrous. I suggest you stop fighting and let him take care of you. It'll be faster that way."

AVERY FUMED THE ENTIRE way back to the launch and then to the *Amphitrite*, which was anchored several hundred yards out from the island. Her mood was not improved when, after depositing her onto the seat at the back of the boat, Knox pretty much ignored her as he spoke with Asher.

The man wasn't dumb. He knew he'd irritated her with that stunt as they'd left the island and was probably trying to give her space to cool off.

Fat chance.

Although, if she was honest, Avery would admit his high-handed tactics weren't all that was stirring her emotions. She was frustrated that they'd been interrupted and apprehensive about returning to the ship.

What was it that Knox had said on the island? Something about returning to reality.

Her reality wasn't precisely great. The pressure of Mc-Nair was back now that she'd survived being marooned. And the thought of damaging Knox and his business weighed even heavier than it had before.

Avery felt torn and restless. Achy and upset.

Things didn't get any better when they returned to the ship—Knox walked off with Asher to speak to the captain.

It was what she'd needed, some space. So why did it bother her so much? Why did she suddenly feel dismissed and used?

She shouldn't, considering she was the only one who'd had an orgasm, but that didn't stop the emotions.

Shaking her head, Avery went to her cabin to wash off the dirt, sweat and sand that felt as if it had been imprinted straight on to her skin. Somewhere between shampooing her hair and pouring body wash onto her loofah, she came to a decision.

Knox might be irritating, but she was going to take her cues from him. She needed to get her head back in the game and off the man's unbelievable abs.

Pulling on clean clothes from the tiny closet, she dried her hair, smoothed it back into a slick tail and fought hard to find the equilibrium Knox had driven away with his wicked tongue.

There was something soothing about the familiarity of the rolling deck beneath her feet when she emerged a little later.

The ship chugged steadily to the northeast, heading back to the dive site. They'd lost time, but that couldn't be helped.

A deep voice startled her. "There she is." Her heart kicked against her ribs before settling back down when she realized it wasn't Knox who'd walked up, but Asher.

"Feel better, Firecracker?" Asher asked, stopping next to her.

"What's with the nicknames? Can't remember my name?"

Asher chuckled and winked, and she relaxed for the first time since they'd discovered that box floating in the middle of the Caribbean.

Why couldn't she react this way with Knox? When Asher flirted and teased it seemed easy. Probably because she knew he didn't really mean it. Something told her his banter was instinctive.

On the other hand, Knox didn't even have to say anything to have every muscle in her body tightening with anticipation and a need she didn't want.

"I know your name just fine, doc."

Avery sighed. "I think I prefer Firecracker."

His mouth curled up into a brilliant smile, the corners of his eyes crinkling with humor.

Taking her by the arm, Asher led her back to the stern. They both leaned against the railing there.

The engines churned, kicking up a foamy wake. At any other time, the view would have been brilliantly beautiful, a hot sun sinking into the sea, spilling pink, purple and orange across the sky and water.

Asher put one arm against the railing, getting nearer to her than was comfortable.

"What are you doing?"

"Conducting a little experiment. Why don't you help me by scooting closer?"

"And why would I do that?"

He shrugged. "Because you're a scholar searching for the truth."

Something told her Asher was up to no good and that the last thing she should do was help him. But she felt compelled to do what he'd asked anyway.

Reaching out, Asher snagged the end of her ponytail dripping over one shoulder. "You wanna tell me what happened on that island, Firecracker?"

"Why don't you get your hands off of her, Ash?"

This time the rough voice behind had her jumping and jerking away. Guilt rushed her. She was fairly certain it was written all over her face. Which just irritated her, because she had nothing to feel guilty about.

Asher leaned close, whispering, "Interesting," so that only she could hear.

She wanted to ask him just what he meant, but didn't

have the chance. Knox wrapped a hand around her upper arm and urged her beneath the shelter of his arm. Her shoulder collided with his chest. Her hand landed on the soft curve of a well-defined pec.

And she had to fight against the urge to sigh and melt into him. It would be so easy to just…stay. To let Knox take the weight of not only her body but the pressure of everything she'd been dealing with the past few days.

But that wasn't her. And it wasn't fair to him.

Planting both palms on his chest, Avery pushed back. "Knox, let me go."

He did, taking a deliberate step back. Her body swayed forward, instinctively moving to close that gap again.

Nope, wasn't going to happen.

She turned, intent on pulling Asher back into the conversation, shamelessly using him as a buffer, but he was already gone.

# 9

KNOX HAD NO idea why he'd grabbed her close. It hadn't been a conscious decision, but an impulse.

He'd looked out across the deck to find Asher cozied up to Avery, his head bent in her direction as they'd quietly talked, and something inside him had just…snapped. Again.

"So what's the plan?"

Knox stared at Avery for several seconds before her question actually sank in.

"For the dive on the wreck? We're heading back to the site right now. It should probably take us about three hours to arrive. Luckily we'd almost completed the sonar scan of the site before we were interrupted."

Avery's single raised eyebrow called into question his choice of words, but Knox chose to ignore her.

"The information we transmitted back to the *Amphitrite* has already been analyzed. We got enough data to verify the wreckage hasn't shifted any more since Jackson was last down. I'm hoping to be diving on the site by tomorrow, late afternoon."

Turning, Avery draped her arms over the railing and stared out across the empty water.

"Where exactly are we?"

Knox found himself standing beside her, mirroring her relaxed pose although he was anything but.

This close to her, that spicy-sweet scent of hers filled his lungs. It was stronger today, and made him want to lean the slightest bit closer so he could bury his nose in the soft cloud of her hair. Although first he'd have to pull it out of that damn tail. After seeing her hair down on the island, he didn't like how she bundled it up, always trying to confine it.

He liked the silky texture, the way it swayed around her shoulders, curling against the curves of her breasts.

"The island we were left on was off the eastern tip of Cuba, between Turks and Caicos, and the Bahamas."

"Why the heck did they take us that far?"

"I have no idea."

At the time he'd known the drug runners were moving them in the opposite direction of the nearest islands, but he hadn't known precisely where they'd been until Asher had rescued them.

It was only one of the things that didn't make sense about the events.

He knew most criminals would have shot them and dumped their bodies rather than going to the trouble of taking them to a deserted island. And while the interruption had definitely knocked their dive off schedule, dropping them that far away must have also affected the drug runners' own plans.

It made him uneasy. His time in the SEALs had taught him that when the pieces didn't add up there was usually a reason. He just had no idea what it was in this case.

And he didn't have a whole lot of time, with pressing issues to worry about—like the fast-approaching deadline for Avery's report.

Avery frowned, leaning farther out over the water. She went up on her toes, her thighs and calves flexing beneath her creamy, smooth skin. He remembered having her legs spread wide for him…

"Did you contact the authorities?"

Shifting to hide the evidence of his arousal behind the railing, Knox tried to focus on the conversation.

"I called a couple contacts in the DEA."

A shiver racked her shoulders. If he hadn't been watching her he might have missed it. "I keep thinking about those guns pointed at us."

He did too. "The entire situation could have been a lot worse."

Avery closed her eyes and pulled in a harsh breath. "I need to put it out of my mind. Think about something else. I tried to look at the research Jackson and Loralei provided, but I couldn't concentrate."

If he knew Avery—and he was beginning to believe he might—she'd already gone over the information multiple times.

"You've read their notes. You've listened to them both. Explain to me how you can doubt that the wreckage is the *Chimera.*"

Avery's shoulders stiffened. Gone was the woman who'd finally begun to relax around him; the ice queen was firmly back in her place.

"Loralei and Jackson are very obviously convinced, but it's my job to find physical evidence that will prove or disprove their findings. The wreckage wasn't found in any of the suspected locations. That, paired with McNair's information about another ship that supposedly went down in the area, casts doubt upon its authenticity."

"After one hundred and fifty years of searching with

no results, it really isn't that surprising that the wreck was somewhere no one had previously considered, is it?"

She made a humming noise that could have been agreement, but the frown on her lips suggested that wasn't how she really meant it.

Gripping her arms, Knox applied gentle pressure until she turned away from the water and faced him.

She was so small. It was something he shouldn't have easily been able to forget, and yet, until he towered above her like this he did. Maybe it was the air of authority she wrapped around herself like armor. It hid so much, more than he'd initially realized.

"Explain it to me, Avery." He kept his words soft and coaxing. "Make me understand."

There was a huge part of him that wanted her to say something—anything—to dispel the unease that filled him whenever he thought about her reasons for being on the *Amphitrite.*

She stared up at him out of those ice-blue eyes, sharp enough to cut straight through a man. Knox was beginning to fear the damage she could do to him.

"I'm just trying to do my job. Please, let me."

Her words were a plea that had his heart thumping uncomfortably inside his chest.

And when she pulled away from him, he let her go. Because chasing her right now wouldn't accomplish anything but leave him with more frustration and questions.

God, everything was a jumbled mess. Instead of easing the tension between him and Avery, touching her, watching her come, had only jacked it higher.

But now there was an edge of desperation that he was intelligent enough to fear. He'd thought he could handle bringing her pleasure and walking away.

Apparently he'd been wrong. He wanted her now more than ever. Craved the taste of her on his tongue.

But that couldn't happen, and the conversation he'd just had with her highlighted the reasons.

She was hiding something. He could sense it. While they'd been stranded it had been easy to push his concerns to the side and focus on survival.

But that was no longer the case.

Needing something to take the edge off, Knox grabbed a beer from the fridge in the galley. Asher walked in behind him, and it was obvious he wasn't simply searching for a cold one.

Resigning himself to whatever shit was about to be flung in his direction, Knox popped the top off a bottle and offered it to his friend.

"So, do you want to tell me what happened on that island? The good doctor is being tight-lipped."

"Nothing."

Asher raised the bottle to his mouth, condensation sliding down the side as he leveled a stare at Knox. "Yeah, you can bullshit with the best of them. But don't forget we're practically family. And I know when you're lying."

Knox wasn't the kind of guy to kiss and tell. Asher typically had no compunctions about sharing his sexual conquests over beer and burgers, but that just wasn't Knox. Today, however, he felt the urge to unburden…mostly because he needed someone to talk him out of making things worse.

He was restless and itchy, the way he'd get right before a major mission. His skin felt tight, as if it was a size too small.

"We…had an interlude."

Asher let out a laugh. "Seriously, man? Interlude?" He drew out the single word, making it sound idiotic.

"Shut it."

Knox paced across the galley, pulling huge gulps of beer as he went. The alcohol wasn't helping.

"Dammit! We didn't even have sex. Not really."

Asher snagged his arm, stopped him cold. He cut a hard glance at Knox, studying him for several moments.

Gone was the affable guy, replaced by the soldier who had covered Knox's ass on multiple occasions. It wasn't a side Asher showed the world often, at least not outside the pressures of combat.

"Please tell me you didn't screw this entire thing for us by breaking your own rules. I told you to get close to her, but sleeping with her probably wasn't smart."

"We didn't have sex…exactly," Knox answered, his voice tight.

"Exactly?" Asher's mouth twitched. "You losing your touch?"

"No! And she'd agree with me."

Asher's eyebrows rose. "Oh, that's how it went, huh?"

Shit, he hadn't meant to admit that much.

"When the hell are you leaving?" Knox asked. "Thanks for the rescue and all, but shouldn't you be heading for the Great Barrier Reef about now?"

His friend laughed, the sound scraping against already raw nerves. "One of the guys is taking me to the mainland tomorrow so I can catch a flight to Australia."

Knox seriously hoped the flight was long and uncomfortable.

"The real question," Asher said, throwing him a pointed glance, "is what are you going to do?"

What could he do? They were on a deadline, with only a little over a week left for Avery to authenticate the wreck. Losing those two days had the potential to screw them royally. If they couldn't provide the US courts with concrete proof by then, they were likely going to lose their permits and any chance of ever salvaging the *Chimera*.

That was his fault and something he'd have to live with. Not to mention bust his ass to make up for.

Avery had had a gun pointed at her head and they'd both lost days of work neither could afford.

Even counting all that, it was hardly the worst he'd ever messed up. No, that was reserved for the night his brother had died.

"Since you took the locating beacon from the boat, we can't track it." Asher mused.

"Hey, I made the best decision I could at the time."

"Chill, man." Asher held up both of his hands in surrender. "I'm not questioning your decisions—well, at least not that one. Just stating a fact. We can't track the runners that way, or recover our equipment."

He really didn't have time to focus on catching the drug runners now, but he would eventually. It might take a while, but Knox was going to make damn sure those guys paid for threatening Avery and leaving them both stranded. He was a patient, patient man.

"They'll make a mistake. Criminals always do."

Though Knox had gotten the impression these weren't your average criminals. In fact, the man in charge had been slick and confident, might even have a military background. It was definitely worth checking with some contacts.

In the meantime, he had bigger fish to fry.

As much as it pained him, they were going to have to call it in and let the proper authorities handle tracking down their boat. It wasn't as though he ever expected to see the thing again. Losing the boat hurt, but not nearly as much as losing the expensive sonar equipment that had been on board.

Knox swore, then drowned the rest of the foul words he wanted to let loose with another huge swallow of beer.

"So, Romeo, did you at least uncover something interesting about the good doctor?"

Knox's shoulders stiffened. Asher wanted intel. It was understandable. He'd been alone on a tropical island with Avery for over twenty-four hours. They'd been in a high-stress environment, which tended to bond people quickly. He'd seen it time and again with soldiers in the field.

Was that what was going on between them?

He didn't think so. He'd been attracted to Avery Walsh long before that island. Being stranded had simply forced them both into a position where they couldn't ignore the attraction anymore.

But it rubbed him the wrong way that Asher assumed he had ulterior motives for what he'd done with Avery. And he certainly didn't want her to think that.

"She told me quite a lot," he said slowly. She'd revealed pieces of herself, both by words and actions. Especially once alcohol had entered the equation. She'd shared deeply personal stories about her past, her sister. "Nothing relevant to our situation, though."

Or he didn't want the details she'd given him to be useful. His stomach turned at the thought of taking such a tragic incident, her sister's struggle with addiction and subsequent OD, and using it to wiggle his way into the truth.

With anyone else, he wouldn't have thought twice about the ethics involved. But with Avery…it was clear she didn't let many people close. He wasn't ready to twist the trust she'd placed in him for his own gain.

Not yet.

But he was afraid that's what he would have to do eventually.

"It's clear she's hiding something," Asher said.

Knox frowned. "Yes."

Asher sent him a pointed look. He knew what his friend was going to say before he even opened his mouth, and there was a part of Knox that wanted to hate him for the suggestion.

He didn't want to use sex to get the answers they needed.

But it bothered him that he cared so much about protecting her. She should have been nothing more than a means to an end. A quick way to get what Trident needed so they could all move forward with this salvage and make enough money to keep them going for years.

Luckily, they were interrupted by Ben, their captain, before Asher could make the suggestion he anticipated.

"There you two are. I've been looking for you everywhere. Thought you'd want to know. They've issued a hurricane watch for Puerto Rico, Dominican Republic and Haiti. Depending on the track of the storm, they expect to upgrade that to a warning within the next twelve hours."

Brilliant. He was seriously starting to believe this dive was cursed. Maybe he could blame Jackson for removing the bracelet he'd recovered from the floor of the *Chimera* and given to Loralei.

"How is this storm going to impact us?"

"Well, it might not at all. It's possible the system could shift."

Knox didn't like the deep grooves marked into Ben's face.

"If it doesn't…?"

"It looks to pass right over the *Chimera's* location."

"How long?"

"A few days, depending on the storm's speed."

"Shit." The *Chimera* was already unstable and perched precariously at the edge of a ravine. Even if the storm didn't make a direct hit, it could seriously disrupt the ship's resting place.

He let out a few choice swearwords. Asher joined in, his face going grim.

"We better call Jackson."

*HE WAS GOING to hurt her.*

*The thought was clear in Avery's mind. Panic and darkness pressed in, smothering her just like the hand spread wide over her chest.*

*"You are so soft and beautiful," the deep voice murmured in her ear, the words smooth and yet somehow menacing. A hand traveled up the curve of her thigh, stroking her skin in a way that had dread coiling tight in her belly.*

*She was disoriented, darkness and sleep making her brain sluggish.*

*"Who? What?" she managed to gasp, blinking, scrambling.*

*Fingers tangled in her hair, tugging hard and holding her in place as she tried to scoot away from the figure towering above her. Tears stung her eyes from the fear and the pressure. Strong fingers dug into her skin at the waistband of her shorts.*

*He moved into the dull light spilling through a small crack where the door opened to the hallway. Recognition blasted through her, settling some of her trepidation.*

*"Melody's room is one door down." She wanted to tack on,* you idiot, *but bit off the words. Her sister's creepy—and probably high, drunk or both—boyfriend had slipped into the wrong room.*

*But the relief was short-lived because he didn't move. Instead, he pressed closer.*

*"I've been watching you. For weeks now, I've wanted you. I see the way your eyes follow me, little one."*

*Panic seized her. A whimper clogged her throat. She tried to pull away, but his hands held her down, crushing her into the soft mattress.*

*He tugged at the waistband of her shorts, jerking them down far enough to expose the sharp edge of her hip bone. His eyes were wild, his breath coming in hard gasps. The stench of alcohol swept across her, strong and sharp.*

*Avery opened her mouth and let out a bloodcurdling scream. The force of his hand hitting her cheek cut off the sound.*

*"Bitch," he growled, pressing his hand down over the bottom half of her face.*

*She couldn't breathe, but he didn't seem to care. Not even when her fingernails started ripping at his wrist, desperate to claw him away. She kicked, but her legs were tangled in the covers and the shorts that were now down around her thighs.*

*Something exploded. The hands holding her down were ripped away.*

*Her father had yanked him off, was beating the shit out of the boy. Her mother hollered. Melody screamed. An explosion of light and sound crashed in on her as her entire world collapsed in one brief moment that she hadn't asked for.*

*Suddenly, instead of watching in horror as her father's knuckles crunched into the boy's face, she saw the tiny black hole of a gun staring at her, held by a shadowy figure with a twisted smile.*

*Wait. This wasn't right.*

*The man staring down at her wasn't the boy who'd attacked her so many years ago, but the man who'd stolen their boat and left them stranded.*

*The guns were all pointed at her again. And Knox. He*

*was going to do something stupid, heroic, and get him-*
*self shot.*

*"You should have stayed safe on that little island. Now*
*I'm going to kill you. Hurt you both."*

*Avery heard the scrape of metal against metal as he*
*squeezed the trigger. Instinct had her rolling sideways,*
*dropping from her bed to the floor even as another scream*
*clawed out of her throat.*

She hit the hard floor with a thud that jolted through
her bones. The door exploded inward, bouncing off the
wall with a reverberating thud.

Knox stormed in, dropping into a low crouch.

"Avery. Are you all right?"

She blinked, taking in the way his calculating gaze
scanned the room, cataloging it in seconds.

Her heart thudded in her chest. Her skin was clammy
with sweat. And she couldn't catch her breath. It had been
a hell of a long time since she'd had a nightmare.

She didn't like it. But liked it even less that Knox had
found her, sprawled on the floor in terror over memories
her subconscious had twisted together.

Slowly, Knox stood, unfolding above her. Wearing
nothing more than a pair of athletic shorts slung low on
his hips, he was gorgeous. All compact muscle and tanned
skin. Just as deadly as the man who'd haunted her dreams.
And yet she wasn't afraid of him. At least, not physically.

Her eyes traveled from his bare feet, over tight calves
and massive thighs to the delicious V that arrowed down
beneath his waistband, and up to those shoulders that she
was certain were broad enough to carry the world.

For the first time, Avery realized she was still spread
across the floor. Elegant. Trying unsuccessfully to hold
back a blush, she pushed to her hands and knees.

Before she could gain her feet, Knox was right beside

her, his hands wrapped around her upper arms to hold her steady.

They straightened together, inches apart. She could feel the heat of him sinking into her system in lovely waves.

But she didn't like the way he stared at her, concern, confusion and disquiet all jumbled up together inside his golden-brown eyes. Because behind those emotions, she could see all the questions swirling.

"Dammit," she breathed out. It had been a very long time since she'd let those memories break free in her dreams. Years, actually. That night had been scary, but she hadn't been hurt, not really. The damage to her life had come afterward, the attack starting a domino effect that had ended with her sister in a permanent-care facility.

But this nightmare had been different. Maybe it was the unfamiliar surroundings or the events of the past two days that had brought about the mishmash of memories.

Blinking again, Avery realized Knox still had his hands wrapped around her upper arms. He was so close—the clean, musky scent of him filled her nostrils with each stuttered breath she managed to pull in.

Knox gently guided her back until her knees connected with the edge of the bed and she collapsed onto the forgiving surface.

Her gaze never left his as he released her arms and crouched down in front of her.

"Are you hurt?"

Now that he'd asked, Avery realized her elbow throbbed and her knees stung. She'd hit them both on the floor. The back of her head ached. She must have hit it on the edge of the bed in her fall. Without thinking, she reached up to rub the spot. She'd barely registered the slight lump there before Knox was pushing her hands out of the way to probe her scalp.

"Ouch." Avery winced and tried to move away, but Knox's hand clamped onto her shoulder, holding her in place. "Stay still."

"It's nothing. I bumped my head."

"You have a knot."

"I know. And let me just say having you poke at it isn't making it feel any better."

He pulled away from her. Avery appreciated the few inches of breathing room he'd put between them. But the reprieve didn't last long.

Grasping her face, Knox placed his thumbs beneath her chin and tilted her head back. Rising, he loomed over her, leaning close.

The position mirrored the nightmare she'd just had, enough to send a burst of adrenaline into her system.

"What are you doing?" she asked, her voice scratchier than she wanted it to be.

Applying gentle pressure, he angled her head this way and that, staring straight into her eyes. Restless energy joined the kick of adrenaline, combining to make her twitchy and…needy. He was so close. She could reach out, place her hands on his hips and pull him between her open thighs.

But she didn't.

Even if she really wanted to.

"I'm afraid you may have a concussion."

"I don't. I'm fine." She edged back, as much for her sanity as anything else. She was too foggy and vulnerable for Knox to have his hands on her right now.

Part of her was happy when he let her go, but she couldn't quite fight down the tiny trill of disappointment that shot through her system.

He took a single step backward, although the pull of his gravity didn't lessen quite enough for her peace of mind.

A smile twitched at the corners of Knox's mouth. "Don't think I've met anyone over the age of five who's fallen out of bed."

Avery's skin flamed pink again. Embarrassment quickly morphed into irritation. "I didn't fall." Okay, so technically she had. "I had a bad dream. I was trying to escape a man attacking me in my own bed. Rolling out seemed like a good response at the time…until I actually hit the floor."

The humor that had been lurking in Knox's expression faded away. "I'm sorry. Do you want to tell me about it?"

She shook her head.

"Take it from someone who's been there, it helps."

He didn't wait for an invitation, but dropped onto the bed beside her. The hard length of his thigh brushed against hers. She wanted to press into him, which was why she scooted away.

"Don't tell me you have nightmares, big, bad SEAL."

He leveled her with a stare, intense yet with an edge of vulnerability that had her belly flipping.

"I've had a recurring nightmare since I was sixteen. The night my brother, his girlfriend and my best friend died. I'm driving the car, like I was that night. Sometimes it's just as I remember it, the deer coming out of nowhere. The heavy thud as it connects with the bumper. The inhuman squeal and crack of bone. The slick roads. Losing control of the car and skidding, rolling over until we came to rest at the bottom of the ditch on the side of the road. Blood and screaming. Holding my brother's body, tears dripping down to mix with the blood soaking his shirt as I wait for the paramedics to arrive."

Avery's breath caught in her chest, stalling there and making her ache. The hitch in Knox's voice didn't help.

Or the way he stared straight into her, unflinching as he detailed the events of that night in a calm, even voice.

But she could see the pain lurking deep inside his gorgeous eyes.

"Bethany died on impact. She was thrown from the car and came to rest about ten yards away. I pulled Chase from the car first. His face was covered in blood, but he was conscious. In so much pain. I left him on the side of the road to go back for Kyle. I'll live for the rest of my life with the guilt of knowing my best friend died alone. And that my brother lingered in pain for hours before he finally lost the fight."

Oh, God. Her heart was breaking for the boy he had been, the man who still carried the scars of that night.

"And that's bad enough. But it's so much worse when my mind turns on me, playing out a scenario that ends much differently. On those nights, it takes a few minutes to remember Kyle is still dead when I wake up."

Avery shook her head. A heavy weight settled in the center of her throat, preventing her from saying anything. Because, really, words wouldn't help anyway. The best she could do was lean close and offer him the warmth of her body as comfort. Her arm slipped around his waist, her forehead colliding with the curve of his shoulder.

There was something about the story he'd just shared, the quiet guilt and despair he couldn't hide, that had her opening up rather than shutting down…the way she normally did.

Avery wasn't the kind of person to confide. Her childhood had left her isolated, constantly moving, being surrounded by people speaking a different language and living a different culture. She'd tried to fit in. She'd been curious enough to learn as she went. But being naturally on the shy side, it was always easier to hang back and view things from the periphery.

From the moment she'd met Knox McLemore she hadn't

been able to do that. Their first angry encounter had broken through her typical reticence. And the residual animosity had pulsed between them, fueled by sexual tension and physical awareness ever since.

Now she had no idea how to backpedal.

"When I was sixteen, my older sister's boyfriend tried to rape me."

She felt his body stiffen. He was a rock-solid wall of male aggression, even if that energy was tightly leashed. He didn't make a sound or move, but he didn't have to. So close to him, she could sense the throb of his hostility. Luckily, she knew it wasn't actually aimed at her.

"Tried?" The single word was low and tight.

"Yes, my father stopped him. But that night changed everything, for me and my sister."

Avery remembered those weeks and months. Worrying about Melody, wondering if she'd used the ticket her parents had given her to fly home. If Avery would ever see or hear from her sister again.

Melody had been so angry—at everyone, but especially at Avery.

"We moved back to Texas afterward, my parents deciding that moving around had contributed to my sister's wild streak. We'd been back off and on over the years, but it didn't feel like home. Although no place really did. I fought them when they tried to send me to a public high school. I didn't want to come into an unfamiliar environment so close to graduating. So I threw myself into finishing as quickly as possible using an online home-school program and started applying for early admission to colleges."

Needing some separation from Knox in order to tell the small white lie that was about to come out of her mouth, Avery leaned forward. She propped her elbows on her knees and ducked her head, her hair swinging forward as a kind of barrier between them.

"Melody OD'd my last year of grad school. She'd been arrested for selling drugs several years before. My parents disowned her then. They went so far as to tell people I was their only daughter. They refused any calls from her. She'd made too many mistakes and they weren't willing to forgive her."

It had been difficult to watch her parents turn their backs on Melody. Avery hadn't been able to do that. Not at the moment Melody had needed her most. She'd spent day and night at the hospital, refusing to let Melody give up either. None of the doctors were optimistic about her sister's prognosis, but Avery believed.

If there was one thing she knew about her sister, it was that Melody was a fighter.

Avery needed to get off this subject before she either revealed too much or Knox saw more than she wanted.

"So, the nightmare started out a replay of that night, but somewhere in the middle it morphed into what happened with the drug runners."

She shivered.

"You were solid when that happened. Steady as a rock. I was impressed. I know soldiers who would have lost it back there. But you were cool. Kept your head."

"Thanks," Avery couldn't stop the smile that tugged at her lips.

Knox's opinion shouldn't matter, and yet it did. His praise sent a warm flush through her system.

"But that doesn't mean the experience can't haunt you days, weeks, even years later. Listen to what your subconscious is telling you, Avery. Don't hold that fear inside. Let it out."

She nodded. He made sense. She just didn't know how to follow through on the suggestion.

Offering comfort, his arms wound around her shoulders, pulling her tight against his body.

She expected him to say or do something, but he didn't. Instead, he simply held her. It took several moments for her own body to relax, melting against the hard, comforting planes of his.

And maybe because he didn't ask, the words started flowing.

"I've always been awkward around men," Avery said, her voice soft and low.

"I find that hard to believe. You're one of the most confident, competent women I've ever met."

"The pearls, heels and suits are armor. They're easy to hide behind."

His fingers threaded through her hair, gently urging her head back until she was looking up into his face. "I don't think so. Maybe they started out that way, but now they're who you are."

"Maybe I don't want them to be who I am." Maybe she no longer wanted to be the stiff, remote woman everyone seemed afraid to approach. When she was younger, the walls she'd built had protected her, from embarrassment, awkward situations and the anxiety that came with putting herself out there.

But the longer those walls were up, the lonelier she became until one day she'd realized she was utterly alone, with nothing but her work to show for her life.

She'd devoted everything to Melody. Even when she had a few days away from the demands of her job, she spent them with her sister. Up until recently, she hadn't even been certain Melody cared that she was there.

In the past eight months, Melody had been getting better and better. On her last visit they'd sat quietly together, watching movies. And when she'd gotten up to leave, Melody had offered her a hug. The kind of blind affection she hadn't known from her sister since they were both little girls.

Avery wouldn't trade anything in the world for those moments. But that didn't chase away the loneliness.

Why didn't she feel any of that with Knox? With him she wasn't lonely or anxious or cautious. With him, she felt as if she could finally be herself.

"You have a reputation, Dr. Walsh. One you should be proud of. You worked hard to earn it."

Avery choked on her guilt, uneasy dread mixing with unexpected pride. To hear him praise her work was a victory, especially since he'd fought so hard against having her on the team. "Says the man who didn't want me here."

Knox chuckled, his breath stirring the hair at her temple with moist heat.

"Your qualifications were never my concern."

"Mmm. So, what were your concerns?"

"The same ones I still have. You're hiding something, Avery. It makes me uneasy. I don't trust you."

"And yet you had no problems putting your mouth all over me on the island."

With her back snuggled against his chest, she felt his body's reaction to her words. His erection pressing into her hip.

"I can separate business and pleasure. My question, Avery, is can you?"

# 10

THREE DAYS AGO he hadn't known this woman, not really. And he sure as hell hadn't trusted her—still didn't, if truth be told. But apparently that wasn't stopping his drive to protect.

The moment he'd heard her scream rip through the quiet night, he'd been out of bed and down the hall. Instinct rather than intelligent reaction.

Knox was enough of a soldier to realize there was a time and a place for both, but it bothered him that he hadn't stopped to think before racing in. That kind of blind response could have gotten them both hurt if Avery had been in real trouble.

And the fact that he thought that a possibility said quite a bit. He had no idea what she was hiding, but it wasn't good. He had to be prepared for anything.

He hadn't intended to say he didn't trust her, but the words had simply come out.

There was a part of him hoping she'd use the opportunity to come clean with him. But she didn't.

Instead, she wiggled in his lap, rubbing her rear against the burgeoning ridge of his erection. Sucking in a harsh breath, Knox tightened his fingers around her hips, attempting to hold her still.

But she wasn't having any of that.

Twisting out of his grasp, she scooted off the bed and turned to face him.

She studied him, those pale blue eyes chasing across his face. He could read the hunger there. Felt an answering response as it grew.

"Yes," she finally said, her voice breathy. He wanted to hear her raspy cries again, to drink them in and claim them as his own.

Knox wasn't sure he believed her. But he also wasn't sure it really mattered any longer.

She was here, standing in front of him, asking for more. And he was fresh out of the control needed to ignore the offer.

Swallowing, she took a step closer, placing her palms on his shoulders before sweeping them down across his chest. Until that moment he'd forgotten he was half-naked.

His hands settled at her hips, fingers slipping beneath the hem of her cotton tank to find the soft skin of her belly beneath. He needed more.

A tentative grin tugging at her lips, Avery pushed him backward. When he complied, she climbed onto the bed, pressing a knee to the mattress on either side of his hips.

She settled onto his lap. His erection, caught between them, throbbed with desperation to be buried deep inside her. A delicious heat radiated from her, soaking into him, the thin shorts she wore offering little barrier.

This time, he had no intention of denying himself what he wanted most. He only had the strength to be noble once.

Sweeping the dark red strands of hair over her shoulder, Knox exposed her throat. Going in, he pressed his hot mouth against her skin. She was so soft and fragrant, like vanilla and flowers.

She sighed, the sound echoing between them, and tipped her head back to give him better access.

He wanted to savor this experience. To relish the trust she was placing in him by letting go this way.

Tugging at the delicate strap of material on her shoulder, Knox bared more of her skin. Trailing with his mouth, he sucked and worshipped, paying special attention to every pulse point he encountered until she was breathless in his arms.

And then he did the same thing on the other side, unable to tear his gaze away from the sight of the soft material that caught on her tight nipples before slipping down her body to pool in her lap.

There was something gratifying about the glazed expression on her face. The realization that he could make the entire world disappear for her with nothing more than his mouth and hands was powerful.

But there was so much more.

Lifting her up, Knox rolled them both, spreading her out across the bed. She tried to reach for the long ridge of his erection, but Knox didn't let her get a hold. Gripping her wrists, he held her arms over her head, wrapping her fingers around the edge of the headboard.

"Don't let go."

Avery whimpered a protest, but didn't move.

A grin stretched across his lips. This was going to be highly enjoyable…for both of them.

Picking up the trail where he'd left off, Knox worked slowly down her throat, across the hollow of her collarbones to the distended peak of one nipple.

Her back arched, silently asking him to lick and suck. But he wasn't ready for that. Instead, he blew a soft stream of air over her and watched as she writhed at the caress, which was too delicate to assuage the ache building inside her.

"Please, Knox," she groaned out, her fiery gaze following his every movement. "I need…"

Her voice trailed off, but the words weren't necessary. "I know exactly what you need, angel."

Knox pulled one nipple into the heat of his mouth. She bucked, her hips seeking more. But he didn't let up the pressure. Instead, he ran just the edge of his teeth around the hard knot.

Her chest rose and fell with shallow, ragged breaths as he gave the same attention to the other side. His own body was on fire, his skin tight with the urge to rush, to claim what he wouldn't let himself have just last night.

But he wasn't going to do that to her. Tonight he intended to savor every cry that fell from her lips, every shiver that passed through her body and every demanding clench as the tight fist of her sex squeezed him.

He could feel the tension winding tighter inside her, drawing her muscles taut. The scent of her arousal permeated the space between them, heady and hypnotic. He wanted more of it.

Stepping back, he grasped the edge of her shorts and tugged them down her body. Her legs scissored, telling him she craved more.

But he wanted to look at her.

Standing at the end of the bed, Knox let his gaze travel down the length of her body. Avery watched him, her eyes glassy, swollen mouth parted as she tried to pull in enough air.

He understood. She took his breath away too.

"God, you're gorgeous."

Knox noted the erotic flush of her creamy skin, the

lithe, compact muscles her extensive time in the water had given her, the delicate cast of her features and the exotic coloring of her hair and eyes.

This time, he started at the arch of her foot. Trailing his mouth across her instep, he enjoyed the way her toes flexed at the caressing tickle.

She whimpered, laughed and then groaned.

Alternating nipping bites and soothing kisses, Knox worked up her calf to the sensitive hollow behind her knee. Her inner thigh. He didn't even have to coax her legs to open. By the time he reached the V where her hip and thigh met she was panting once more.

Restless. He knew exactly how she felt. He'd never wanted a woman so much in his life.

But there was more to this than just sex. Yes, he wanted her with a desperation that bordered on madness. That wasn't all, though. He wanted to hear what her life had been like growing up with archaeological digs as her playground. What her hobbies were. What kind of music she liked.

Avery was strong and independent. Talented and intelligent. The kind of woman who wouldn't hesitate to put him in his place and yet still somehow managed to be delicate and draw out his protective instincts.

And if he didn't suspect she was keeping secrets, he might be tempted to fall at her feet right now and promise that he'd worship her forever.

But he couldn't do that. So he settled for finishing what he'd started instead.

HER BODY WAS going to go up in flames if Knox didn't take her. Right. Now.

She might be a bit shy, but when she wanted something,

Avery was a force to be reckoned with. And she wanted Knox McLemore.

Pushing against his shoulder, she urged him to roll onto his back. She followed, rising above him in a way that had a powerful, unfamiliar sensation surging through her body.

She had this gorgeous man willingly at her mercy. It was something she'd never thought she wanted or needed, but with Knox…he made her feel perfect and powerful.

Avery wanted to make him as mindless with need as he'd just made her. She wanted his blood to pulse. To have what he hadn't given her last night—all of him.

Working the gym shorts over his hips, she freed his impressive erection. She'd felt the hard length of him pressed against her body, but seeing it…was so much better.

A pearl of moisture welled at the tip before sliding down. Avery took her fingertip and spread the drop, slowly caressing down the taut length of him.

He hissed, his hips pulsed and his hands fisted into the sheets.

Knox was perfection, but she wasn't just talking about his body. Sure, the layers of muscle melded together to create an undeniably amazing landscape, but the smaller details were what caught her eyes.

The curve of his shoulder and the twist of black ink that ran across his back. The V at his groin and the tattoo of a frog skeleton that flowed up from it and was only visible now that his clothes were off. The tiny pucker of flesh several inches above and to the right of his belly button. The jagged scar along his right side.

The evidence that he'd spent years putting his life on the line, placing himself in harm's way so that others wouldn't have to. Noble. Honorable.

The kind of man every woman would want in her life and bed.

And she had him, gloriously, perfectly naked.

Crawling back between his open thighs, she swept her hands down over the solid wall of his chest. With delicate strokes, she paid homage to the various scars and marks across his body with her mouth.

She enjoyed the way his muscles contracted wherever she touched. The sheen of sweat that popped up across his body as he attempted to remain still while she did whatever she wanted.

Damn, the man was something else. Contained. She respected that kind of discipline. Even as she could see the need roiling faster and faster as he watched her with that hungry gaze, he didn't rush her.

She'd never expected that kind of physical and emotional control to be a turn-on. But it was. Because it showed her, without a doubt, the kind of strength this man possessed.

It wasn't something he bragged about. Or flaunted. It just was. A part of him he most likely didn't even think about.

But she did.

Avery let her eyes dip down his body, much as he'd done to her. She might have felt exposed in those moments, but something told her Knox was perfectly comfortable inside his own skin. That confidence was what set him apart, what made him uniquely frustrating and appealing all at the same time.

Her focus dropped to his sex and she couldn't help herself. She swiped her tongue across her bottom lip.

"Avery, you're killing me here. Show a little mercy, woman."

She smiled as she stared up into his blazing eyes. "I don't think you really mean that."

"Suck me, touch me, ride me, I don't really care which,

but you have about thirty seconds to make up your mind before I do it for you."

His words were low and even, but the promise in his eyes sent a thrill racing through her.

She wanted all of those things, but right now what she wanted most was to feel him deep inside her.

Positioning her thighs on either side of his hips, Avery rose above him. The expression on his face was gratifying as he followed her every move.

Wrapping her fist around his erection, she stroked up and down several times. He was hot against her palm. Smooth and hard at the same time. She ran the pad of her thumb up over the head, pleased when his eyelids fluttered and then narrowed with warning.

The man beneath her was powerful, dynamic. He could easily have done whatever he wanted with her. And there was no doubt in her mind that she'd pushed him to the very end of the leash on his control.

There was something exciting about that knowledge.

But she didn't want to risk pushing him anymore.

"Condom?" she asked.

"Bedside drawer," he growled back.

It didn't take her long to reach over, rummage around until she found a stash and then roll the tight ring of latex down over him.

But the delay felt like a lifetime. They were both panting by the time Avery brought him to the entrance of her body. She pressed down, taking him inch by inch. The twinge and pull as she stretched to accommodate him was exquisite. The slide of him against her swollen, aching flesh felt amazing.

She was torturing them both now, although she'd really been doing that all along.

Their groans mingled when her hips met his, finally

taking him all in. Avery sat, unmoving, soaking in the sensations that bombarded her senses.

She could practically feel his pulse where they connected. Or maybe that was her own body.

Rising on her knees, Avery let him slide out, almost to the very tip before plunging back down again.

Fast, slow, she rode him, never taking her gaze away from his. She wanted to watch as his world fell apart, just as hers had last night.

Placing her palms on his chest, Avery braced herself as she picked up speed. Her lips latched onto the underside of his jaw, kissing, licking, biting.

More, she needed more. The orgasm was building. She could feel the sharp edges of it, but couldn't quite reach it.

The room spun around her, but she refused to stop. Her own heartbeat thudded fast and loud against her eardrums.

His fingers tangled in her hair, holding it away from her face so he could get a clear view of her. Her entire focus was him, them. And the way he watched her…she couldn't have looked away even if she'd wanted to.

She felt his body winding tighter and tighter beneath her, pushing up with each of her downward thrusts, trying to steal just one more inch of pleasure and connection.

But she couldn't let go.

Seeming to sense her building frustration, Knox gripped her hips and flipped her onto her back. He loomed above her, blocking out everything and drawing her world down to just him.

It was exactly what she needed.

"Touch me, Knox. Please."

He simply grinned at her, his expression going feral with promise.

He did a hell of a lot more than touch. Wrapping one

arm beneath the bend in her knee, he pressed it up and out as he slipped deep inside her.

Avery's breath caught as she arched up into the pleasure. She should have felt open, exposed. But she didn't. How could she, with the way Knox was looking at her? As if she was the only solid thing left in the universe.

There was no build to the orgasm. One minute it was too far away and the next her body was imploding. She couldn't control it or the way she shouted his name, not caring who might hear on the quiet ship.

The world spun out and for several moments she felt weightless, the same glorious sensation she'd only ever found beneath the water.

It was breathtaking. Profound in an unexpected way. Sex had never been earth-shattering for her. She'd had friends over the years gush over one lover or another. She'd listened as colleagues shared tales of their exploits.

She'd never had that.

Until now.

Even delirious, she felt the kick of Knox's release deep inside her as he joined in the ecstasy. And that only increased the experience, the mingled moments of pleasure shared. Energy flowed between them.

A knot of something clogged her throat. Avery swallowed it.

Knox collapsed onto the bed beside her, rolling them both so that she faced him, and tucked her comfortably against his body.

She felt boneless. "I'm pretty sure I'll never be able to use my legs again. How the hell can you move?"

His palm spread wide across her rear, squeezing and pulling her even tighter against him. He made a sound, a cross between a grunt and a rumble of approval. "One of us deserves a gold star from the professor."

Avery chuckled, burying her nose against his shoulder. He was warm and a little sweaty. He smelled like man, which, as far as she was concerned, was perfect.

"Pretty proud of yourself, aren't you sailor?"

"That's frogman to you."

"Mmm," Avery murmured, stretching her body.

She felt him relax. Really relax, all the tension leaving his body and melting away into nothing. Until that moment she hadn't realized just how…alert Knox always was. Even the night before when he'd held her in the sand, it had been there. Now she recognized the difference.

Avery wasn't sure whether to be flattered that he was comfortable enough with her to let go, or feel guilty because he probably shouldn't.

Because now that her physical hunger had been met, the tug-of-war she'd been fighting with her conscience was back in the forefront of her mind.

This didn't help. She shouldn't have given in, but it was too late now. Actually, it had been too late the moment they'd been forced onto that tiny island together.

It didn't take long for Knox's breathing to quiet and sleep to claim him. Unfortunately, her own mind wouldn't stop churning.

How was she supposed to do what McNair wanted after what she'd just experienced?

But how could she not? If she didn't say the wreckage wasn't the *Chimera*, McNair would ruin her reputation. Without that, her opinion as an expert would be devalued…worthless. She'd lose her business, her home, her life. Melody would lose access to the care facility that was finding a way to help her.

She would hate herself if she followed through. But did she really have a choice? She wouldn't be able to live with herself if her choices left Melody helpless.

There was no good answer. No way out.

Despair pulled at her, thickening the lump that had stuck in her throat.

She'd woken up afraid of a nightmare, but Knox had chased that fear away. Unfortunately, there was no one who could save her from the destruction she was about to bring upon herself.

# 11

KNOX TRIED NOT to stare as Avery walked across the deck of the *Amphitrite*. But the woman was difficult to ignore, especially in a wet suit. He'd touched and tasted every inch of her body and lived in a perpetual state of wanting to do it again.

That damn wet suit put everything on display even if she was covered in neoprene from neck to toe. Every delicious curve was outlined and he wanted them all to himself.

It didn't help that he wasn't the only one who noticed. He'd caught several of the men staring across the deck, whatever tasks they'd been performing completely forgotten.

Avery, on the other hand, was oblivious, which only made her sexier.

When she'd first strode across the deck in her pearls and heels he'd thought she dressed that way for the attention. It hadn't taken him long to realize that was the furthest thing from the truth.

And considering the story she'd shared with him after her nightmare, he understood why she used clothing as a facade, a kind of armor. She projected a sense of confidence that she didn't always feel. Which floored him.

Avery Walsh was one of the most intriguing, beautiful, dynamic women he'd ever met. She was complex in a way that called to him, stirring a need to dig deep beneath those layers and understand what made her tick.

They were diving on the wreck today. He'd organized a group that would inspect the structural integrity of the ship to determine what safety precautions would need to be implemented as they undertook the salvage. They'd be taking measurements, photographs and documenting with video.

He planned to shadow Avery as she made her own assessments, recording and cataloging what she could from outside the wreck. That was as close as he planned to let her get today, until his team could evaluate the risk of going closer.

Avery wasn't going to like being held back, but they would both have to live with that until the ship was stabilized.

Striding across the deck, Knox fought the urge to bend her back and kiss the hell out of her. It was impulse and need, an unfamiliar compulsion he didn't necessarily like.

And he knew Avery wouldn't appreciate it if he made a spectacle of her in front of the entire crew.

But that didn't mean he had to keep his distance.

Although if he was smart he would, if only to protect his own reputation. The last thing he needed was for someone to discover he was sleeping with their nautical archaeologist.

Not that he would try to get her to alter her report if she decided the wreck wasn't the *Chimera*, but he didn't need McNair or anyone from the US courts believing he could.

Reaching for the tanks she'd dropped at her feet, Knox began inspecting the lines.

"What are you doing?"

He didn't even bother looking up. "My job."

"No," Avery drew out the single word. "You're doing my job. That's my equipment. My safety responsibility."

Crouched down at her feet, Knox angled his gaze up at her. Okay, so he took a little longer than necessary to find her icy eyes, enjoying the detours along the way. "You're on my ship. Your safety is my responsibility, Avery."

Her jaw tightened, a minuscule tic picking up the corner of her mouth. "I don't see you inspecting anyone else's gear." She leaned closer, whispering for him alone, "Are you doing this because you're sleeping with me or because you're afraid I'll slip something down there to sabotage you?"

He was smart enough not to react to her words, because she would surely use whatever he said against him.

Although apparently it didn't matter because her fists landed on her hips as she glared at him. "No, really. I've been diving for a hell of a long time. I know what I'm doing."

"My business partner was trapped down there, Avery. Almost couldn't get out."

"So? I'm not Jackson. I don't take unnecessary risks with my life."

Why had he needed to hear those words from her so badly?

Select members of the team had been down to the wreck since Jackson's accident, but everyone on the crew had been under strict orders to proceed with maximum caution. No one had been allowed close. They'd used robotic cameras to inspect what they could of the ship.

But Avery hadn't been content with the pictures those expeditions had provided. She'd insisted a firsthand view was necessary to collect data, measurements and inspect the ship for minuscule details cameras were notorious for missing, especially in the murky depths.

That hadn't bothered Knox when this whole thing had started, but it did now.

Pushing up from his crouched position on the deck, Knox stared at her. A familiar ache centered right in the middle of his chest, fear and guilt mingled with a powerless frustration because he knew there was no way to prevent her from going down there.

It was dangerous. He didn't like the idea of her being close to that wreck. But Trident needed her down there.

Avery stalked close, snatching her regulator out of his hands. He'd forgotten he was holding the thing.

"If this is your passive-aggressive way of trying to get me out of the picture again, I'm not amused."

Knox's eyebrows knit. "Of course not."

Okay, so a week ago he might have done or said anything necessary to get Avery off the *Amphitrite*. But not now. Not after they'd been stranded together, bonding over shared rodent and fireside confessions. Not after he'd touched and teased her, learned the breathy sound she made as she came.

"Look, you're good at your job, Avery. I've always thought that. I didn't agree that we needed anyone to authenticate the wreckage. Jackson and Loralei spent a lot of hours sifting through historical records, ocean currents and hurricane data. They knew exactly where to look to find the *Chimera*. McNair's claim that she's another ship is ludicrous."

"Right, because no one else over the last one hundred and fifty years sifted through the same data? Knox, people have been looking for the *Chimera* for a long time. And considering no one expected her to be resting anywhere near the Bahamas…excuse me if I remain skeptical. McNair presented credible evidence that this could be another ship."

"You haven't seen her."

"Neither have you."

She wasn't wrong. While Jackson, Loralei and some others on their crew had been down, he hadn't had the chance. But he'd seen enough data and photographs to know what they were dealing with.

"Look, the ship is unstable. I'm worried about you going down there. I've seen enough friends injured and bloody, lost enough people who mattered to me to be cautious when someone I care about is taking unnecessary risks."

Avery's mouth opened and then slammed shut again.

Knox didn't realize what he'd said until that moment. Her wide-eyed expression didn't exactly breed confidence.

On top of that, Knox still didn't trust her. He'd been worried someone would accuse him of using his connection with Avery to influence her. But maybe her goal was to distract *him*, deflect his attention from her true purpose. He had no idea what that purpose could be. He wanted to believe she was here strictly to do her job, but his gut told him there was more going on.

"I...I don't know what to say."

Knox closed his eyes, screwing his lids shut for several moments so that he could regain his composure. It had definitely deserted him right now.

His stomach felt as though he'd swallowed an entire quart of battery acid. Had he just made a huge tactical error without even realizing it?

God, he hoped not. There was a part of him that wanted to see how quickly he could reel those words back in. But something stopped him. He'd spent so many years blaming himself for the accident, pushing people away not only because of the guilt but also because it hurt so damn much to open up, to risk caring for and then losing someone.

His unintentional admission made him vulnerable. But he was starting to realize there were worse things in the world, and if he didn't risk something, he was going to be left alone anyway.

Jackson had found Loralei. Asher was gone more often than he was home lately.

"Look, I buried my brother when I was sixteen. I've witnessed plenty of men—on both sides of the line—die. Trust me, when you've been caught in the middle of death and destruction, you become very protective of the people who matter."

She swallowed visibly. "Are you saying I matter?"

He wanted to say yes, but the word wouldn't come.

"I'd be concerned for anyone on my team who was going down there to poke around."

"But you're not inspecting their equipment."

"No. I'm not."

Slowly, Avery nodded, but her eyes never left his. Her tongue snuck out, sweeping across her plump pink lips.

He wanted to kiss her, and this time the urge had absolutely nothing to do with proving a point or staking a claim. He wanted the taste of her filling him up.

"Just promise me you'll be careful."

Her eyes searched his for several moments before she said quietly, "I promise."

Knox wasn't certain whether it should settle his nerves that she'd so easily agreed or jack them up even more.

He was walking a knife's edge with this woman. And he was afraid that when it was over, he would be the one bleeding.

AVERY LOVED BEING in the water. She had to in order to do her job. There was something soothing about the underwater world in which she was often a guest.

Today, she'd need that peace. Unfortunately, it was difficult to come by when Knox flanked her every move.

His hovering would make her nervous on a good day, but this couldn't be considered good.

Avery wasn't sure what to hope for—that she'd find definitive evidence this ship wasn't the *Chimera* or proof that it was.

She knew what Knox wanted. Expected.

And the thought of disappointing him left a sour taste in her mouth. She'd had to be the bearer of bad news on numerous occasions in her career. That had never bothered her before—the facts were the facts, simple as that.

But now she had a conflict of interest, and not only because she was sleeping with Knox.

The team descended slowly, going several hundred feet beneath the surface, the water gradually getting darker as the sunlight could no longer penetrate the depths.

Avery was awestruck at her first glimpse of the wreck.

She took in its power and majesty. The irrefutable evidence of the ocean's destructive forces.

The nature of her job often had her dealing with shipwrecks, remains of ancient civilizations, and underwater tragedies. The power of water to both destroy and give life never ceased to amaze and humble her.

This wreck had been buffeted by winds, swamped by waves, dragged down to the depths of the sea by a storm so powerful it had the potential to toss large ships as if they were tinker toys.

This wasn't the first ship she'd studied that had been destroyed by the force of a hurricane. Without the modern convenience of tracking and warning systems, these kinds of storms would often take ships and islands by surprise, leaving people helpless and alone.

Avery couldn't suppress the shiver that snaked down

her spine. Or stop thinking of the impending storm they'd been briefed about earlier in the morning.

Respect. She could never lose her respect for the sites she surveyed, the windows they opened into other times and other lives.

The ship was huge, looming out of the darkness. Behind it, the water appeared almost black—the abrupt drop-off she knew the team was concerned about.

A jagged hole in the side of the hull was clearly visible. The ship had tipped onto its side when it had landed on the sea floor, indicating to her that it had rolled before sinking.

It was breathtaking. Haunting. Somehow sad.

A tight band pressed against her chest. Avery stopped, treading water as she let her body and emotions catch up.

She always had the same response when viewing these kinds of wrecks. They were graveyards, after all.

And yet there was something uplifting about seeing the ship as well. Against the odds and elements, the thing stood. Maybe not straight, but still surviving, refusing to surrender completely to the sea that had sucked her down.

She felt a kinship with the wreckage. A determination to push through, as always. To tackle the issues in front of her one step at a time.

First, she needed to know for certain whether this was the *Chimera*. Then she could decide how to proceed with McNair's threat.

Knox stopped beside her, laying his hand on her arm. Through the plastic of their masks, he peered at her and signaled, asking if she was okay.

She nodded and gave him a thumbs-up before moving closer to the wreck.

The water was noticeably cooler in the shadow of the ship, but that didn't stop Avery.

It was clear that this was no ironclad steam ship, as most

of the blockade runners had tended to prefer. But then, she'd already known that about the *Chimera*.

She needed a better look, but it was clear the ship was a wooden side-wheel steamer. Probably over 150 feet.

So far, the details matched the information they had of the *Chimera*. But then, she'd found that out from the photographs and video Trident had provided.

What she needed now was irrefutable proof, either that the wreck was the *Chimera* or indicating she was the ship McNair was claiming.

In her mind, Avery conjured up the drawings she'd studied of the *Chimera*, trying to fit the present pieces together with the past. But with the ship lying on her side and so damaged, it was difficult to tell whether or not they matched without getting a closer look.

Avery kicked out, streaming towards the wreck only to come up short when something yanked on her ankle.

Thrashing out, she tried to free herself. Twisting, she found Knox behind her, his hand gripping her foot.

Even through the shield of his mask, she could tell he was glaring at her. She kicked again, harder this time, until he finally released her.

Irritation sizzled through her veins.

Ignoring him, Avery went right up to the hull. She'd read about Jackson Duchane's accident when they'd first made the discovery. She understood the risks and had no intention of putting herself in harm's way. But that didn't mean she had to stay fifty feet back.

She couldn't do her job that way and had no intention of letting Knox tie her hands.

Bracing herself on the edge of a hatch, Avery peered inside. She could feel Knox behind her, tall and forbidding, but ignored him.

Several beams had fallen across an opening opposite

her. To her trained eye, it was easy to spot the newly exposed wood that had been protected for years until Jackson's accident had bared it to the briny water.

Something unexpected caught her attention, but she wanted a closer look to be certain what she was seeing.

According to the information she'd been given, Jackson had been farther into the ship when the bulkhead had collapsed. And by his own admission, he'd knocked his tank against the wall. She'd be careful.

Kicking out, she was mindful not to disturb anything, staying well clear of the debris and walls, and keeping the exit in close proximity in case she needed it quickly.

Pulling the underwater camera out of the pouch tied to her waist, Avery nearly caught her breath at the markings carved into the beams that had fallen.

She snapped picture after picture, her heart thudding.

These kinds of markings were often the difference between identification and speculation. Her dad had often said an archaeologist was part detective, part psychologist, part fortune-teller.

Archaeologists took tiny pieces and fit them together until most of the picture materialized. Often, the smallest items or seemingly inconsequential data made the biggest difference. One marking on a hieroglyph, a single word incorrectly translated, a broken shard of pottery.

These were the moments she lived for. The ones that made her grateful for her job, the excitement and thrill she couldn't get anywhere else.

She wouldn't know for certain until she could better examine the photographs and identify the markings, but it was possible the beams could be traced back to a ship builder and even a ship.

When she was satisfied with what she had, Avery moved carefully back through the cockeyed cabin. Her eyes darted along the trail of debris left by the catastrophe that had sunk the ship.

Pieces of the hull, covered with grime and years of salty crust, were scattered across what had become the floor of the wreckage.

Among the bits of damaged wood, several objects caught her eye. She hesitated to remove them, but the *Amphitrite* was equipped with the tools needed to properly preserve anything they brought up. She fought back unexpected nerves.

Avery had done this a hundred times over the course of her career, why did she suddenly feel like a green archaeologist on her first recovery? Her heart thudded, her skin felt clammy inside her wetsuit.

She didn't have time for this kind of reaction, or hesitation. Carefully photographing the objects for identification and logging, she reached down and gingerly retrieved a round lump of something. She hoped it and another odd-shaped item covered with barnacles and a green crust would prove useful.

Knox's impatience was almost palpable as he glared at her from the doorway. He indicated his own dive computer, wordlessly informing her that they needed to ascend.

She knew precisely how long they'd been down and how much oxygen they both had left. But there was no need to push the man completely past his breaking point.

She already knew she was in for a battle once they reached the surface.

# 12

KNOX WAS PISSED, but there was little he could do about it now. Even down below, short of wrapping his arms around Avery and dragging her back up to the surface like a drowning victim, he couldn't have stopped her from entering the *Chimera*. Which left him frustrated and irritated.

Normally the controlled ascent necessary for surfacing after a dive didn't bother him. He appreciated the need to complete the task correctly.

Today, watching as Avery moved steadily upward, the painstaking care grated against his already exposed nerves. And the longer it took, the more his temper simmered, boiling dangerously close to the surface.

He tried to find that center of calm he'd fought hard to develop during his training with the Teams. Unfortunately, it was nonexistent today. Every time he thought he had a handle on it, the image of Avery disappearing into the belly of the ship rose up in his mind and set him off again.

She'd promised him she'd be careful and at the first opportunity had darted straight off into danger.

Bright sunlight blinded him as they climbed back aboard the *Amphitrite*, but he didn't let the momentary discomfort slow him down. He began shedding his equipment, shoving it into a corner to deal with later.

He ripped at the zipper on his wetsuit. The thing felt as if it was suffocating him, or maybe that was his anger. With jerky movements, he peeled it away until it dangled at his hips.

Stalking across the deck, he grasped Avery's elbow. She didn't jerk away, but coolly looked up at him, her eyes calm and clear.

That didn't help his mood at all.

He was ready to blow a gasket and she was acting as if nothing was wrong.

"Dr. Walsh, we need to have a word," he ground out between clenched teeth.

She pulled in a deep breath, holding it for several seconds before answering. "Yes, I imagine we do, but you're going to have to wait a few minutes."

Grabbing the bag that had been tied to her waist, Avery pulled her arm from his grasp and walked over to talk with Shawn, one of the divers.

Knox followed.

"I need these items cleaned and preserved as quickly as possible, please," Avery said, proceeding to tell Shawn how to log the artifacts, including their location. Knox listened as she provided him cautionary direction on how to handle the delicate items without damaging them.

Shawn nodded as she explained each step she wanted him to follow, then cradled the bag in his hands, peering inside with an expression of wonder and awe.

Certain they were both on the same page, she moved to turn away, but Shawn stopped her, placing his hand on her arm. "I promise I'll take great care with this, Dr. Walsh."

"Avery. Please, call me Avery," she said, gifting him

with a bright smile that Knox noticed didn't quite reach her eyes.

So maybe she wasn't as unaware of the argument they were about to engage in as he'd first thought.

Turning back to Knox, Avery raked him with a cool gaze. He watched her shoulders straighten as she attempted to pull every spare inch out of her limited height.

He tried not to let how cute she was, hair in a wet tail down her back and her body outlined in her tight wetsuit, sway him. But it was damn hard.

Perfect, now his temper was mixed with lust, a highly combustible combination.

Gesturing her ahead of him, Knox indicated she should lead the way across the ship. He wasn't surprised when she chose the room that had been designated as an office instead of her own cabin.

Something told him this conversation was going to leave him frustrated and highly unsatisfied.

AVERY DIDN'T BOTHER waiting for Knox to launch his verbal attack. She cut straight to it, hoping to head him off at the pass.

"I'm sorry."

His mouth opened and then slammed shut again, flattening into a thin line.

Maybe it would have been better to let him bluster and get all the pent-up frustration out in the open. She could see the tension stringing his muscles tight. Could practically feel the vibration of it running through his body.

"What, exactly, are you sorry for?"

Avery crossed her arms over her chest, eyeing him. She could tell him what he wanted to hear, but that didn't quite sit right with her.

"For upsetting you."

"But not for swimming straight into danger."

"I don't recall doing that."

"Then you have a shitty memory."

"Pretty sure there's nothing wrong with my memory."

Knox scowled. The thunderous expression shouldn't have been sexy. Yet her body reacted as if it was.

Her blood whooshed inside her veins. Her nipples tightened and her sex began to throb with a relentless need.

None of that was helpful at the moment.

"I'm not an idiot, Knox. The ship was stable. I didn't go far inside and I was constantly aware of my surroundings."

"A lot of good that would have done if the thing had shifted again and the ceiling had come crashing down on your head like what happened to Jackson."

"From what I read, Jackson was partly responsible for that."

Knox rolled his shoulders, his mouth pulling into a tighter line. "Maybe."

"Look, there's no sense in arguing about this. We'll have to agree to disagree. Either way, hopefully I have what I need to make a determination, with the photographs I took and the artifacts I recovered."

She could see the conflict playing out in his eyes, the desire to have things settled against the need to hang on to his anger.

Eventually, practicality won out. It was something she appreciated about Knox, his unclouded view of the world.

"Let me download the pictures and see what I've got. We'll go from there."

"Fine, but you better hope you got what you need, Avery, because it'll be a while before I trust you that close to the wreck again. Not until I've heard from our structural consultants. I'm running a business here and have insurance, safety regulations and the rest of the team to

think about. You not only put yourself at risk but everyone else. If something had gone wrong we would have
had to kick into rescue mode. There were other ways to
get what you needed."

He wasn't wrong, but there was a clock ticking in the
back of her head. She silently admitted it might have
pushed her to do something she wouldn't have normally.

"We're both running out of time, Knox. You know it
and I know it. McNair isn't a patient man and he won't care
about our incident with the drug runners, the approaching storm or the instability of the wreck. The courts have
placed a deadline on a determination and he'll insist they
follow it. The longer this takes, the worse the outcome
for Trident."

Avery watched the jumble of emotions spin through
Knox's eyes—frustration, acknowledgment, the sharp
edge of unresolved anger—before he spun on his heel.
He didn't bother slamming the door behind him, although
she knew he probably wanted to.

It might have been better for both of them if he had.

Avery didn't like the idea of anyone influencing the way
she chose to conduct her work. She already felt trapped
enough by McNair. She didn't need pressure from Knox
as well.

Dropping into the seat behind the desk, she opened her
laptop and switched it on. She connected the waterproof
camera and it began downloading the series of photographs she'd taken.

Heading to her room, Avery changed clothes and grabbed
her phone before returning to the office.

She probably should have stayed away and let the camera run, but she couldn't stop herself from watching as a
preview of each picture popped up onto the screen, one
after another.

Leaning close, she peered at the images, trying to force her eyes into making out the markings. She was going to need to blow them up to get a better look. Impatience crackled through her system. She wanted this over with.

Although at the same time she didn't. Because when it was all said and done she was afraid of what she might lose—her career, Knox, everything.

Avery was on edge, which was probably why her entire body jolted when the cell phone she'd placed at her elbow began to vibrate against the tabletop.

*Unknown* scrolled across the screen.

Normally, she wouldn't bother answering an unidentified caller, but considering everything that was going on she hit the green button to pick up the call...and then wished she hadn't.

"Dr. Walsh," came a rich, smooth voice that had the ability to make her skin crawl.

"Mr. McNair," she answered, keeping her tone level to hide her jolt of fear. Nothing good could come from this call. "What can I do for you?"

"You can tell me you've uncovered evidence the ship is not the *Chimera.*"

Avery bit the inside of her cheek, forcing the words she wanted to scream at the man to stay behind her teeth. When she was certain she had control over her tongue, she said, "I'm sorry, I can't do that."

"And why not?" She could hear the censure in his voice. It left her feeling unsteady.

"Because we encountered a problem and I only began diving on the ship today. However, I took some photographs and retrieved a couple of items that I'm hoping will help me make a determination. As soon as I do, you'll be the first to know."

"Ms. Walsh," McNair said, emphasizing the *Ms.* "I'm

certain you're aware that actually doing your job isn't necessary in this situation."

"You might not think so, Mr. McNair, but I do."

"Suit yourself, my dear." His condescending and artificially sweet tone had a tingle of unease tripping down her spine.

McNair had her backed into a corner. Powerless. She'd felt the same way, watching her sister self-destruct and knowing there was nothing she could to do to help.

"You know the outcome, I expect. Do whatever you must in order to deliver it. Because I'd really hate to see you lose the career you've fought so hard to gain. And how would your sister fare at a state-run institution? Even at the best facilities, accidents happen all the time."

Avery couldn't hold in her gasp. Her hands began to tremble, the phone shaking against her ear.

It was one thing for McNair to threaten her, but Melody…her sister was helpless. And while the facility had security, she didn't doubt McNair could find a way in if he wanted to get to her.

What was so important about this damn ship that McNair would go to such lengths to interfere in Trident's salvage?

At first she'd assumed he wanted the gold. That had to be it, right? But there was no guarantee the gold even existed. It was possible the story had been fabricated and embellished over the years, as often happened with legends. The gold wasn't listed on any manifests, but it wouldn't have been, considering the plantation owners were trying to smuggle it to the Confederacy.

No one would know the truth until they could get the wreck stabilized enough to salvage whatever remained inside the hold. The Trident team hadn't even been able to get robots in to take photographs.

She'd aided in the recovery of almost twenty sunken vessels over the years—some had yielded more data, artifacts and treasure than expected. And some had held none.

It was a gamble. A high-priced one considering the cost of the equipment, man-hours and energy involved in recovering a ship like this one.

She never considered the monetary gains from salvage. For her it was always about discovering and preserving artifacts that provided valuable insights into human history. But McNair clearly didn't value such things.

It might help if she understood what drove him, but she really didn't. And without that piece of information she was walking blindly into a fight she knew she couldn't win.

"Ms. Walsh, don't make me provide additional motivation for your cooperation."

Before she could respond, a loud tone buzzed obnoxiously in her ear telling her McNair had hung up on her.

Picking up a glass that had been left on the desk, Avery sent it flying toward the far wall. The crash was more therapeutic than she'd expected. Throwing things wasn't her normal MO, but she'd needed an outlet for the flash of frustration-drenched anger and the glass had been handy.

Her chest heaving, she stared at the shards glittering in the late-afternoon sunlight streaming through the porthole high on the wall.

Unfortunately, her satisfaction was short-lived when the door burst open and for the second time in as many days, Knox rushed inside, his eyes darting around the room until they finally landed on the mess.

His body slowed and those rich brown eyes came to rest on her. "What the hell happened?"

How was she going to explain this?

AVERY STOOD IN the middle of the room. Her eyes were blazing, her skin flushed pink with anger. Her chest rose and fell, drawing his attention even as he tried to push the awareness away. Now wasn't the time.

"Well?" he prompted.

"Nothing," she bit out.

They both knew that was a lie.

"Bullshit, Avery." He took several steps closer, but stopped when she backed away. He didn't want to pressure her, but he wanted an answer. He couldn't fix what was wrong if he didn't understand.

"Tell me what happened."

She looked at the desk, the porthole, the broken glass, everywhere but his face. Yet another sign that she was hiding something. One of many.

He watched emotions chase across her face—desperation, hope, resignation, despair. Whatever was going on, it was big.

But he'd already known that.

Knox held his breath, feeling stupid for hoping she'd trust him and finally tell him the truth.

"I got a phone call."

His heart thudded painfully. Maybe. Maybe.

"Your sister?"

Her ice-blue eyes finally jerked up to his, looking him squarely in the face. "No. Melody is fine."

At least that was something.

"For now," she whispered, so low that he wasn't sure he'd heard her correctly.

"Tell me."

She shook her head. "There's nothing you can do. Drop it, Knox. Please."

He moved toward her, using her retreat against her until her back collided with the bulkhead.

She stared up at him out of those gorgeous eyes, the mix of fear, regret and caring in them nearly driving him to his knees. "Just tell me it has nothing to do with the *Chimera*."

Her throat worked. "It's personal," she whispered.

He didn't believe her, not entirely. But what could he do about it? Not much.

Frustration and worry twisted in his gut. It was a combination he didn't particularly like.

Spearing his hands into her hair, Knox tipped her head back so he could stare deep into her eyes. "Don't lie to me, Avery. Not anymore."

She simply shook her head, pulling the strands around his fingers tight to the point that it had to be tugging on her scalp, not that she seemed to notice or care.

Going up on her tiptoes, she brought her mouth to his. The kiss started tentatively, the slide of her lips hiding the passion he knew ran deep beneath her calm surface.

He could have taken over, but he didn't want to. He wanted to feel her need grow until it overpowered that hesitation she couldn't quite shake. He wanted something from her, if she wasn't going to give him her trust.

If he was smart, he'd walk away from her. But he couldn't. He was just now starting to realize how tangled he was over this woman. Definitely in deep.

The frenzy hit hard. He watched it glaze her eyes, flush her skin. Her tongue darted across the seam of his lips, asking and then taking what she wanted.

She was using it against him, the fervor she caused in his blood.

But he couldn't seem to stop, even knowing it would most likely end up causing him a hell of a lot of pain.

Right now, all he cared about was the pleasure they could give each other. The reprieve they both apparently needed.

# *13*

GOD, WHAT ON EARTH was she going to do?

The thought twisted through her brain, but she let it get swept away by something better. The feel of Knox pinning her against the wall with the hard press of his body. His mouth on hers, the bitter taste of beer mingling with chocolate-chip cookies. Catherine must have baked while they were diving.

She needed for Knox to help her forget how screwed up her life had become.

It was selfish and stupid, because she knew it wouldn't solve anything. But she wanted it. Besides, wasn't it well past time for her to be a little selfish?

Her entire life, she'd put everyone around her first. She'd been the good child, because her parents had had their hands full with Melody. She hadn't tasted her first beer until she was twenty-one. She hadn't sneaked out like other teenagers to do stupid things.

She'd put her career in jeopardy because someone had needed to take care of her sister. And now she was considering a deal that would crush her soul but save Melody once again.

She hated herself for even contemplating it, and yet she pretty much knew what she was going to do.

So, she deserved a few hours of selfishness.

The restless, helpless feeling that had been building inside her to the point of explosion had a new focus—Knox.

Clasping her hands behind his head, she brought him back for another kiss, letting that familiar snap turn into a rushing burn. She welcomed the sizzle of it across her skin, the way her need for him expanded, filling every cell of her body until it was a living, breathing, demanding thing.

He groaned, the vibration of it tickling against her skin.

Grasping her around the waist, Knox boosted her up so that her back was tight against the wall.

The heavy ridge of his erection nestled perfectly against her throbbing center. They were both wearing too many clothes.

She wanted fast and furious, needed mindless and overwhelming right now. But he refused to give it to her.

"Please, Knox," she begged against his mouth, nipping, biting, arching her hips in an enticing way to tempt him into giving her what she wanted.

He simply shook his head, using the thrust of his hips to hold her still against him.

Gathering both of her wrists in one hand, Knox pinned them above her head. His mouth found hers again, pressing heavy kisses to her already swollen lips, sweeping his tongue inside, teasing and chasing, before pulling back out again.

"Slow down, baby. There's no rush."

That's what he thought. She needed the passion only he could make her feel to wash away everything else.

If he wouldn't hurry, at least she wanted the feel of his hot skin against hers. Avery flexed her wrists, testing his hold.

Knox chuckled, the vibration of it rumbling across her skin where his mouth ghosted down her neck. "I've had years of training, have close to seventy-five pounds of muscle and almost a foot of height on you. Do you really think you can break my hold?"

Smirking, Avery stilled, taking his words as a challenge, even if he hadn't meant them that way. She hadn't needed her martial arts skills in a while, but that didn't mean she couldn't handle a little wrist grab.

Knowing that the element of surprise was on her side, she pushed her hands forward, forcing an inch between them, before jerking back and down, bringing her elbows tight together and driving both of their connected hands down.

Knox moved with her, a grunt of surprise slipping out.

She twisted into his body, using the motion and his weakened grip to rip her hands out of his hold.

Waving her fingers—now free—at him, Avery said, "Did I forget to mention I studied Muay Thai in Thailand?"

She wouldn't have been surprised to see annoyance clouding his face, but enjoyed his grin of appreciation a hell of a lot more.

"You really are full of surprises, aren't you, Dr. Walsh?"

The tiny bubbles of euphoria that had begun to effervesce inside her burst all at once. But Knox didn't seem to notice. "I'll have to remember that the next time I need to blow off some steam. You're a hell of a lot more fun to spar with than Asher."

Snagging her around the waist, Knox pulled her close again, latching his lips onto the skin at the curve of her throat. His mouth continued to slip across her body, leaving a moist trail of fire everywhere he touched.

God, she needed to feel him. Avery pulled his shirt off, baring his tanned skin to her hot stare. She traced the line of muscle. Through her clothes, he sucked the aching peak of a breast deep into his mouth.

She wanted nothing between them, but couldn't find the words to convey the thought.

Knox worked his fingers down, popping the catch and zipper on her shorts and pushing them down over her hips. Avery kicked when they pooled at her feet.

He lifted her off the floor. For a moment she thought he might sweep the desk clear and spread her out across it. Wanted that gritty, intense experience.

Instead, he settled them both in the big leather chair behind the desk. Her thighs spread wide, squeezing around his hips.

The hard ridge of his erection pressed against her, hitting just right. Oh, hell. He felt so good. "More," she pleaded, writhing on his lap.

"Avery," he said, his voice rough. His hands swept across her cheeks, jaw and forehead. He brushed the wisps of hair that had fallen around her face out of the way.

He held her there, staring straight into her. And for several seconds Avery felt more exposed than she'd ever been in her life, not physically naked, but completely bare.

Until she realized he wasn't just taking, but giving as well. Because as vulnerable as she was right now, he was just as open. And that helped settle her.

She shifted, letting her body rub against him. Heat flared deep in his eyes, flashing golden through the rich brown. A knowing smile curled at the edges of his lips. "Witch."

Reaching for his hands, she pulled them away from her face and wrapped his fingers around the hem of her shirt, holding them in place. They both knew he could pull out of her grasp anytime he wanted, but he didn't.

Slowly, she dragged their hands up her body. The backs

of his fingers skimmed her skin, a touch that didn't go nearly deep enough.

His gaze moved across her, eating up each inch of revealed flesh as if it was a gift. With Knox, maybe it was.

Together, they threw her shirt across the room, but Avery didn't release his hands. She guided him around her back and waited for him to pop the clasp of her bra. Each strap fell from her shoulders and it slid to the floor beside them.

With their fingers twined together, Avery directed his hands to her belly. She couldn't hold in the fluttering sigh at the feel of his touch. She guided him across her body. Her head dropped back and, eyelids heavy, she watched his expression from beneath her lashes.

Her entire being heated and hummed. She wasn't certain when he took over and began leading, not that it really mattered. The combined sensation of the pads of her own fingers caressing her skin and then his, hers, his... It was overloading her brain.

Knox caught one tight nipple between his thumb and her index finger, rolled and tugged. A line of electricity zinged from that point straight to her core. Her internal muscles contracted, empty and unsatisfied.

Somehow, one of his hands worked free, sliding up her back to tangle in the heavy hair at her nape where she'd let it free. He held her still, applying pressure until she was looking down where he teased her.

"Watch," he muttered right before leaning forward and pulling her distended nipple into his mouth, right along with her finger and his thumb.

His tongue scraped across both. Avery gasped at the barrage of sensations. Soft, hard, rough, wet.

Her hips moved, unconsciously seeking relief for the

building pressure. His hand swept down her back to settle around her waist.

She wasn't entirely certain which one of them fumbled to push her panties away. Not that it really mattered. Somehow she found herself on her feet, swaying and blinking rapidly as Knox stared up at her from his position in the chair.

He tugged at her panties until she was naked, then quickly removed his own clothes. Pulling a condom from the back pocket of his jeans before tossing them away, he rolled the ring of latex over his beautiful erection.

Hands bracketing her hips, he guided her back onto his lap.

His skin burned against hers, the heat of him searing through her. Her hands settled on his shoulders, sweeping down over the hard ridges and planes of his chest, abs, ribs. He jerked when she touched an unusually sensitive spot, but didn't try to stop her.

And when she finally wrapped her fist around the hard length of his erection, Knox let out a groan, half torture, half relief.

She wanted to play, but craved something more.

Somehow she found the words to say, "I need you."

Grasping him, Avery brought the thick head to the slippery entrance of her body and sank down.

"God, you feel so good," she moaned, taking him deep.

He chuckled, the sound thready and strangled. "I was just about to say the same thing."

Grasping the back of the chair for leverage, Avery rose up onto her knees. The chair tipped back, putting them both off center. Like her world didn't already feel as if it was spinning off axis...

His arms wound around her, holding her, supporting her, guiding her. Over and over again, she pumped her hips, letting him slip almost completely out before plunging back down.

They were both panting. Sweat pearled her skin. Tension coiled deep inside her belly, deliciously tight.

"You're killing me," Knox said, fingers digging into her skin.

The chair rocked with the force of their joined thrusts. His powerful hands gripped her, moving her in perfect time, hitting the spot inside that only he seemed able to find.

The orgasm exploded out from her center, making every muscle contract and quiver.

"Oh, my...Knox," she managed to utter. Her fingers hurt where they gripped the chair, but she didn't care as she rode out the powerful wave of her release.

Despite feeling as if every bone in her body had been replaced by jelly, she tried to hold herself upright. It was a Herculean effort, but worth it when she got to witness the sheer pleasure and relief that washed across Knox's face. The way his eyes rolled back, every muscle in his body went rock solid and his mouth opened on a moan of satisfaction.

She'd done that to him.

Together, all useless limbs and sweaty skin, they collapsed against the worn leather. The chair rocked and creaked.

"I don't think this chair will ever be the same," Avery whispered. Her head snuggled just below the damp line of his jaw.

Knox tried to smother his laughter, but failed miserably.

Contentment, an unfamiliar feeling for her, bubbled up.

Unfortunately, even completely blissed out, she knew it couldn't last.

AVERY TRIED NOT to think about what had happened in the office yesterday, but it was difficult not to be distracted.

Despite those memories, the office had become her sanctuary. All around her, the crew was in a tizzy. In the night, the hurricane had changed track and was now heading straight for them.

The dive that had been scheduled for today had been canceled. They were busy preparing to find shelter in Nassau.

The captain had woken Knox in the middle of the night. Neither of them had been particularly happy since they'd only been asleep for a couple of hours.

If she hadn't been groggy, she might have been amused by the captain's embarrassment and surprise at finding her in Knox's bed. Apparently their relationship wasn't a secret anymore.

As it was, she'd needed copious amounts of coffee to kick her brain back online. Knox hadn't fared much better. While he was completely in control, over the past week she'd become intimately familiar with his body. She could easily read the tension riding his shoulders, the worry lines tightening the corners of his mouth.

Unable to do anything productive above decks, Avery had decided it would be best to get out of the way and let the rest of the crew do their jobs. So she'd holed up in the office and buried her nose in research.

First, she tackled the photographs she'd taken, blowing them up and running them through enhancing software in an attempt to sharpen the markings carved into the beam. She'd almost crowed with triumph when after about two hours of painstaking work, the words had become clear.

Realizing time was against her, she emailed the enhanced version to a colleague in the UK, asking for some information.

The *Chimera* had been commissioned and built over there and she hoped someone more familiar with the maritime industry in that time period would be able to quickly identify the markings.

She'd been careful not to mention the project she was working on, and felt guilty for that tiny lie of omission. But the last thing she needed was for someone else to identify the ship before she'd decided how to handle McNair.

Then she began to dig through websites, research sites and online libraries.

She was in the middle of a break—standing with hands braced at the small of her spine, leaning back, in an effort to work out the knots that had tightened there—when a heavy knock sounded against the door.

Before she answered she knew it wasn't Knox. He wouldn't have bothered requesting entrance to his own office.

"Come in."

She was surprised and excited to see Shawn, the guy she'd passed the two artifacts from the wreck to the previous day.

"I thought you'd want to know, we've made progress on the pieces you recovered."

"That was fast." Not only was the process of preservation a painstaking one, but with the impending storm Avery had assumed everyone would be pulled to other duties.

"Mr. McLemore requested we work as quickly as possible. We're all anxious to have the ship authenticated so we can begin excavation."

"I hope you followed protocols to protect the pieces."

"Absolutely, Dr. Walsh."

Gesturing for him to lead, Avery said, "Let's take a look." She slipped into the hallway and back up onto the deck. In a far corner, the artifacts she'd collected were soaking in two clear acrylic boxes. She knew the solution surrounding them was a combination of water and chemicals that would help gently remove the deposits caused by being submerged in salt water for a hundred and fifty years.

Neither artifact was ready for display, but there were enough areas shining through the grime that perhaps she'd be able to identify one or both of them.

The man beside her vibrated with excitement. "We think the round item you recovered is actually a small trinket box. We'll have a better idea in a few days. But I thought this might be useful."

Shawn gestured to the far box. It was small, but then so was the piece she'd retrieved. No bigger than the center of her palm.

"We still have some work to do." He leaned forward, practically pressing his nose to the clear acrylic. "But we've uncovered enough to know the item is metal, possibly bronze. At first, because of its odd shape, we worried that it was broken, but as we removed more layers, we realized it's simply unusual."

Avery leaned close and nearly gasped when she realized what she was looking at.

The item still sported a lot of grime, but it was obvious to her that she was looking at a US commemorative medal, given to only a handful of high-ranking members of the US military...including the captain of the *Chimera* before he joined the Confederate cause.

Shit.

Her stomach churned. Her knees went weak and Avery had to grasp the edge of the table to keep herself upright.

There was a small chance the medal belonged to someone else, but in her heart, Avery knew. How many of these commemorative medals could be lost at the bottom of the Caribbean? To her knowledge, only one.

"Are you okay, Dr. Walsh?"

"Yes." The single word trembled, so she tried again. "Yes, I'm fine. Thank you for letting me take a look at these. I'm hopeful we'll be able to get more information as the pieces go through the cleaning process."

She had a little time, but not much. It wouldn't be long before someone else would be able to identify that medal as well. Hell, even an undergrad archaeology student would be able to do an internet search and figure it out.

Which made what McNair wanted her to do virtually impossible. Without such irrefutable evidence she might have had a hope of convincing everyone the ship wasn't the *Chimera*.

Her stomach rolled and bile stung the back of her throat.

Now, even if she lied, the best she could do was gain herself a few weeks before Knox and the rest of the team from Trident realized what they had...and what she'd done.

Maybe she could convince McNair this was a battle they couldn't win.

# 14

KNOX STALKED ACROSS the deck, raking his hands through his hair and pulling some out as he went.

Seriously, they were cursed. There was no other explanation. First drug runners and now a hurricane.

They were never going to get the ship authenticated and evaluated for structural safety. He'd had to make a phone call to Jackson and Asher. Neither man had been happy about the delay, but they realized it was hardly in his control. He was good, but he couldn't force the weather to do his bidding.

Everyone was concerned that if the storm tracked close enough, the surge might dislodge the *Chimera* from her resting place on the edge of the ravine.

None of them were saying it out loud, but he knew they were all thinking the same thing. It would royally suck to have gotten this close only to lose the ship to a freaking hurricane.

That trench was deep, so if the ship moved enough, it was possible they'd never be able to recover her. Past a certain depth they wouldn't be able to dive to retrieve the remains. And there was always the concern that further damage to the structure could scatter whatever artifacts or gold the ship carried across the seabed.

For about five minutes Knox had entertained the idea of putting everyone on the crew down there to open the hold, but that hadn't lasted long. Not even a hold full of treasure was worth putting everyone on the team in jeopardy.

Besides, he was just as interested in preserving the artifacts from the ship as he was in retrieving the gold... although the gold would definitely pay for the privilege of handling the rest of it.

So he'd done the safe thing—the right thing—and ordered the captain to take them to the Bahamas.

He was so caught up in his own drama that he didn't notice Avery was standing in front of him until he collided with her. He grasped her arms to keep her upright as she rocked back on her heels.

"I'm sorry. I didn't see you."

"Obviously," she said, wrapping her own hands around his wrists. "Are you okay?"

"I'm pretty sure that's my line."

He was hoping for a smile, could have used one from her right about now. But her lips stayed flat and even.

"Are you okay?" she asked again, each word deliberate.

"No, not really. I'm worried about the storm. The ship may shift beneath the onslaught and drop into the ravine. And there's nothing I can do."

"Except pray the storm doesn't make a direct hit."

"Yeah, I'm already doing that, but feel free to add your own to the mix. I'll take all the help I can get."

Her grip on his wrists tightened. "You might not believe this, but I really do hope everything turns out okay, Knox."

On the surface, her words were innocent enough, but there was something about her tone that felt off. But he didn't have enough clues to figure out what.

"Thank you," he responded, just as carefully.

"Let me know if there's anything I can do to help." She stepped out of his path, leaving the hallway in front of him clear, sliding one hand down to grip his hand.

"All right. I appreciate that. Ben says we should be in port within a few hours. Kennedy is already working on finding us rooms so we can ride out the storm. Best case scenario, this delays us a few days. Hopefully McNair and the judge will understand and give us some extra time."

"Hopefully," she agreed, though her drawn expression indicated she didn't think that likely any more than he did.

Crap.

He'd been going so quickly, trying to handle so many details over the past few hours, that it hadn't occurred to him to wonder where Avery might stay once they got back to Nassau. Obviously, in their hotel because she was a member of Trident's team and his responsibility but...

"Will you share a room with me when we get there?"

Avery stared at him for several seconds, her ice-blue eyes swirling with some emotion he didn't quite understand. Maybe regret?

"If you want me to."

"I do."

She took a step away from him, the distance between them growing, reminding him of that cold, deep hole yawning beside the *Chimera*.

She let his hand go, her fingers sliding against the inside of his wrist as she continued to move away.

She was halfway down the hall when her quiet words reached back to him, leaving a trail of goose bumps across his skin.

"Let me know if you change your mind."

AVERY RUSHED AWAY from Knox, determined not to let herself look back at his handsome, tempting face.

Shitty timing, running into him in the hallway on her way back from talking to Shawn. She'd needed a few minutes to get herself under control, but she hadn't gotten them.

How was she supposed to pretend everything was okay when she was fairly certain her entire world was about to come crashing down on her head?

But she couldn't tell him, which meant she couldn't let him guess that she was a mess inside. Taking a deep breath, Avery wondered how she'd be able to get through the next few hours, let alone days and nights sharing a hotel room with him.

Knox McLemore saw too much. He'd recognized pieces of her no one else ever had. Things *she* hadn't even realized were there.

Closing the door to the office behind her, Avery leaned her back against the cold plank of wood and twisted the lock at her back.

She grabbed her cell phone, pulled up the last incoming number and pressed it. Her hand trembled as she held the phone to her ear and listened as it rang.

"Ms. Walsh, I hope you have some good news for me."

"No, I don't."

"Well, that's disappointing."

"I found a medal, one that's going to be easily identifiable and almost certainly was owned by the captain of the *Chimera*. There's no way to give you what you want."

Silence echoed down the line, scraping against Avery's already frayed nerves.

"I would have expected an intelligent woman like yourself to come up with some way to explain or destroy the evidence."

Frustration buzzed in the back of her throat. "I can't simply make the damn thing disappear, Mr. McNair. I only pulled two artifacts. It would be immediately missed."

"Then perhaps you should have chosen more carefully, my dear."

God, she wanted to reach through the phone and wring the man's neck. Never in her life had she felt this kind of anger toward another human being, not even her sister's boyfriend. Now, if McNair had been in front of her, she could have joyfully drawn blood.

"You obviously have no idea what you're talking about."

"No, my dear, that's why I hired you."

His words, so silkily delivered, made no sense. "I thought you owned a salvage company."

"I do, but I don't oversee the day-to-day operations."

She didn't understand, but didn't have time to be concerned. "Look. Even if I managed to discredit this artifact, there would simply be another one. The ship is the *Chimera*. I have no doubt about that. Someone will discover the truth."

"Well, that's a shame…for you. I understand the *Amphitrite* is headed to the Bahamas to ride out the storm. Be prepared to headline a press conference as soon as you reach land, announcing the ship Trident found is not the *Chimera*."

"But…" Had the man not heard a single word she'd said?

Before she could formulate another argument, the line went dead. She was really getting tired of him hanging up on her.

This was not good.

McNair would follow through with his plans. Avery had no doubt he would have a full press contingent wait-

ing for them when they reached port, even with the storm
bearing down on everyone.

And he expected her to announce exactly what he wanted.

Walking over to the desk, Avery collapsed into the
chair. She couldn't help but remember how she and Knox
had used it just one day ago.

Right now, that memory twisted in her gut.

She didn't want to betray him, and that was what she
would be doing. But telling the truth would mean losing
her career and putting Melody in jeopardy.

Although, wasn't her career ruined anyway?

She could do as McNair wanted and lie, but eventually
someone would figure out the truth. Her work would be
discredited and she'd lose the reputation she'd spent years
building. Her career depended on that reputation, without
it no one would put any value in her opinion as an expert.

But if she didn't go with the lie, then McNair was going
to expose her secret, reveal that she'd never actually finished her PhD and had been misrepresenting herself for
years. That would completely destroy her reputation. Even
if she went back to school and got the qualifications she
needed, no one in the industry would ever hire her again.

She was screwed either way.

KNOX WAS NOT prepared for the hordes of cameras, microphones and video equipment that met them at the
dock. There was no doubt he looked as if he'd been up
for twenty-four hours, because he had been. His eyes felt
gritty, his skin brittle and thin. He needed a beer, a nap
and to brush his goddamn teeth.

Instead, he was facing perfectly coiffed reporters who
delighted in shoving microphones into his face and hurling
questions at him like, "What are Trident's plans following
the leaked information that the wreck isn't the *Chimera*?"

What Knox wanted to do was grab the mic from a preternaturally perky brunette and throw it into the water behind him. What he did instead was keep his mouth shut. Because he had no idea what she was talking about.

And he'd learned a long time ago it was better to stay quiet until you knew what was going on.

He was about to give some pat "No comment" answer when the crowd shifted. The vultures abandoned him. He would have thought that'd be a good thing, but it wasn't.

Because walking down the dock behind him was Avery, perfectly prepared in one of her high-priced business suits. Her glorious red hair was pulled back into a sleek tail that fell down the back of her navy-and-white pinstriped jacket. Her pristine white heels clicked against the worn wood. And those damn pearls gleamed against her pale skin.

Knox's fists clenched at his sides.

Avery had known this was coming. So why hadn't he?

Stopping several feet away Avery held up her hands. "Ladies and gentlemen, please, let's continue into the yacht club where Mr. McNair has prepared for the press conference. I'll be more than happy to answer any of your questions."

Across the sea of people, Avery's gaze finally met his. Those damn blue eyes. They weren't cold, as he'd expect, but pleading, desperate. Full of guilt.

He wanted to be wrong, but his gut told him he wasn't. Was this what had upset Avery in the office? Prompted her to throw that glass and then jump him as if she couldn't get her hands on him fast enough?

Had that hot interlude all been an act to distract him?

Knox's chest tightened. It ached, just as it had when an insurgent had gotten the drop on him and slipped a knife between his ribs. Luckily, the bastard had missed everything important. Not like Avery…

Crossing his arms over his chest, Knox let everyone sweep past him before snagging her arm and hauling her back a few steps.

"McNair called a press conference," she said softly, pointlessly, since she'd just announced it.

"About what?"

"He found out about the items I recovered."

"That's funny. I'm fairly certain, considering those artifacts are onboard my own damn ship, that I'd know if they'd yielded some definitive answer about the wreck. Wouldn't I?"

She simply shook her head, guilt and sadness clouding her expression.

"I'm sorry, Knox. Just, please."

"Please what, Avery? Ignore the fact that you've obviously been working with McNair behind my back the whole time?"

It was exactly what he'd feared. What his intuition had been screaming from the moment Avery Walsh sat down across from them in the conference room at Trident headquarters.

Dammit, why the hell did he have to be right this time?

Knox shoved away from her, dropping her arm as if it was suddenly coated in poison.

"Go, give your press conference, but know this isn't over."

She swallowed. He tried not to let it affect him that her eyes went watery.

"Dr. Walsh," someone called out.

Knox turned to find McNair standing at the end of the dock, his arm outstretched, fingers open, as if he was waiting to welcome a lover home.

The man was perfectly turned out in a tailored suit.

His skin was tanned and his teeth flawlessly white. The smile he gave them both didn't reach his dark blue eyes.

"Come, Avery, there are people waiting to speak to you."

The command in his voice was hard to miss. But so was Avery's hesitation as she moved toward him.

Knox waited until McNair ushered her down the dock and into a building across the street before pulling out his cell phone and hitting the number for Trident. He didn't bother with a greeting, but said, "What the hell is going on?" when Kennedy answered.

He could hear the tightness in her voice when she answered, "About an hour ago McNair leaked a story that Dr. Walsh had uncovered definitive evidence the wreck isn't the *Chimera* and scheduled a press conference to discuss the particulars."

"That's bullshit."

"Which is exactly what I said to Jackson when he found out about it. By the way, he said to tell you he's sorry."

"For what?"

"Not believing you. About Dr. Walsh."

That was cold comfort right now. And there was more at stake than a little corporate espionage. Knox felt the cut of Avery's betrayal straight down to the bone.

He'd been shot, stabbed and lived through explosions. Having his heart ripped out hurt a hell of a lot worse.

He didn't think he could watch.

"I assume this travesty is being televised?"

"It is."

"Great, because I'm not going to be in attendance."

Kennedy was silent for several seconds before saying, "Okay," drawing out the word into multiple syllables.

"Don't ask."

"Wouldn't dream of it."

"Just…figure out what we're up against so we can formulate a plan of action."

"Will do. What are you going to do?"

There was really only one option that appealed to him at the moment.

"I'm hitting the hotel bar."

It had been a long time since he'd drowned his sorrows in alcohol. Tonight he needed something to numb the pain. Tomorrow would be soon enough to deal with the fallout of this mess.

AVERY COULD FEEL the cut of Knox's gaze as she walked away with McNair, but there was nothing she could do about it.

There'd been no way to warn Knox, not without explaining what was going on. And she'd been afraid. She was going to lose him anyway since she'd been lying to him—by omission if nothing else—since the moment they met.

And if that wasn't enough to cause him to turn his back on her, learning her secret would no doubt seal her fate. He'd condemn her for her choices, as would everyone else.

Until that moment, she hadn't realized just how much she wanted Knox to stay in her life.

The way he'd looked at her, his eyes hard and unforgiving, the pain of betrayal radiating back at her…

It hurt so much.

But she deserved the contempt. She had betrayed Knox and was about to make it worse.

McNair put his hand on the small of her back. She fought the instinct to move away from his touch.

He led her into the room he'd had the yacht club prepare. A dais stretched out in front of her with a podium and several microphones. Chairs were arranged on the floor, quite a few of them already filled with eager media personnel.

"I'm so glad you decided to do the right thing, my dear," McNair whispered into her ear as he handed her up the low flight of stairs.

He stopped several feet behind her and she turned to look at him. There was a part of her that had to appreciate the picture McNair made. He was tall and radiated power in an effortless way. But she knew he wasn't the dedicated businessman he pretended to be.

Her stomach churned sickly as she stepped up to the podium. Avery let her eyes sweep across the back of the room, hoping to see Knox, head and shoulders above everyone else. But he wasn't there.

Her mouth went dry. Reaching for the small glass of water on the edge of the podium, she took a quick sip.

Someone, apparently impatient with her stalling tactics, shouted out into the quiet room, "Dr. Walsh, can you elaborate on your findings and exactly how you determined the ship was not the *Chimera*?"

Avery opened her mouth to force out the words that would forever haunt her, but they wouldn't come. This was a line she couldn't cross. She might have misrepresented her qualifications, but no one had gotten hurt from that choice. She'd been qualified and simply lacked a piece of paper to prove it. This decision would damage Knox and his business. She couldn't do it, not even for Melody or her own career.

Knox might not ever understand or forgive her, but she needed to do the right thing.

She pulled in a deep breath and held it before slowly releasing, trying to find the strength she needed.

"I'm sorry, you were misinformed. The wreckage Trident Diving and Salvage discovered several months ago off the coast of Rum Cay is, in my opinion, the *Chimera*."

A cacophony erupted in the room. Behind her, she felt McNair step forward. She only had a few seconds before he shut the entire thing down.

Leaning toward the mics, Avery raised her voice to be heard above the din.

"Two days ago I recovered a medal from the wreck. Only a handful of men were awarded the honor by the US Congress before the Civil War. John William Ballinger, captain of the *Chimera*, was one of them. I have no doubt that this evidence, paired with the research Jackson Duchane and Loralei Lancaster used to find her, proves the ship is the *Chimera*."

A strong hand wrapped around her arm and yanked. Avery let McNair pull her away from the podium. There wasn't much left to say.

He shoved her into the arms of a hulking man standing behind her. "Get her off the stage," he growled, his eyes cold chips that promised swift retribution for what she'd just done.

The man, obviously McNair's muscle, wrapped his fingers around her arms and dragged her through a doorway behind the dais she hadn't noticed before.

He shoved her against the wall and growled, "Stay," before instructing two more guys to watch her.

Avery rubbed at her arm, certain she'd have bruises tomorrow. Her body slumped against the wall, and she fought the urge to collapse.

Through the open doorway, she listened to McNair ruin her career.

"It has recently come to my attention that Ms. Walsh has been committing fraud for several years. She's been representing herself as a doctor of nautical archaeology when she in fact never completed the doctorate program."

She heard the murmurs and rumblings from the other room.

"Obviously, I didn't learn this information until after she'd been attached to the project. In addition, it's come to my attention that Ms. Walsh has recently become intimately involved with one of the owners of Trident Diving and Salvage."

Her knees trembled, threatening to collapse. How the hell did he know that? The only people who could possibly know that were supposedly loyal to Trident.

Although McNair had gotten to her using her weaknesses against her. Perhaps he'd done the same thing to someone else.

At first she felt sick. She could just imagine how Knox was feeling right now. He'd be pissed that his personal information was being splashed all over the international media.

And that fired up her own anger.

"Given this information, I'll be disputing any findings Ms. Walsh attempts to publish concerning the wreck. Her impartiality and integrity have been called into question."

She was going to give him integrity, right in his face the next time he got close to her. Avery clenched her hands into tight fists.

An unexpected sense of calm settled across her shoulders.

Pushing away from the wall, Avery took several steps back toward the stage, but a heavy hand gripped her arm. Righteous anger had her continuing another couple of steps, pulling against the hold. But that didn't get her far.

She was yanked off-kilter, her body spinning until she

was staring straight into a familiar face, one she'd never expected to see again.

"Hello, Ms. Walsh. We meet again."

The leader of the drug runners stared down at her, a cocky smile twisting his lips and an unnatural gleam shining in his eyes.

What the hell was he doing here? How did he fit into this game?

She didn't have much time to wonder before McNair came striding through the door. He raked her with a hard gaze, then dismissed her.

"Come on," he pointed at one of the other men, indicating the drug runner should follow him.

"What should we do with her, boss?"

McNair paused, his lips pulling into a tight line. "Let her go. She's served her purpose and I don't need her anymore."

With a shrug, a hulking brute with a scar running straight through his top lip, gripped her arm.

She was really getting tired of being yanked and pushed. And if she wasn't outnumbered six to one she might have done something about it, but right now she wanted information.

"Wait," she said when he started pulling her in the opposite direction. "McNair, I don't understand. What is he doing here?"

The drug runner tossed her another grin that didn't hold a speck of humor.

For a minute she thought McNair was going to ignore her. But after a few charged moments of silence, he turned. Walking close, he seized her chin in a grip that would leave marks.

She could smell his expensive cologne, but it couldn't quite cover up the stench of corruption and malevolence.

"You're intelligent enough, Ms. Walsh, I'm certain if you think hard enough you'll figure it out."

"You don't care about the gold, do you?"

The man laughed, the sound chilling her. "No, although I would have taken it. What I need is access to international waters, specifically where I've spent years and countless millions bribing the necessary officials."

"Your diving business is a front."

"And a very convenient one. No one questions a salvage company hauling in unusual cargo."

With that, he turned away, dismissing her.

Frustration, resentment and blinding anger welled up inside her. She couldn't let him get away with this. There had to be some way to stop him.

The two men walked out, leaving her with four more. She didn't doubt the bulges beneath their suit coats were guns. And she really didn't want to have another one pointed at her face.

What now?

"Come on. Mr. McNair said it's time for you to leave."

One of the men grabbed her arm, propelling her forward. Avery stared at the drug runner speaking to one of the other men in the corner. Her mind raced. Maybe with more information she'd hit on something that would help.

The drop zone they'd stumbled on had been very close to the wreck site. Salvaging the *Chimera* could take years. It was a painstaking process where each room would be systematically searched and cataloged. The sea floor close by would even be dredged for artifacts.

McNair had known they were showing up at the site—why the hell had he continued with the drop that day? Was it greed? Audacity? Maybe he'd just wanted to get one more run in before their presence shut him down for a few weeks.

Or maybe…

"Hey," Avery called out, trying to get the drug runner's attention. "McNair set you up."

"What are you talking about?"

"That's the only explanation. Why would he have you retrieve a drug shipment when he knew the Trident team would be arriving?"

The sneer that crossed the man's face had her insides quivering. He took several menacing steps toward her, his expression full of dangerous loathing.

Fear shot through her, but she pressed on. Now was not the time to lose her courage.

"We sent a message changing the drop location, but the idiot pilot didn't receive it in time."

That had been bad luck for all of them, especially since the mistake had resulted in her and Knox being abandoned on that island. Even if everything between them had changed in those few hours.

"Why didn't you just kill us?"

His smile was silky smooth and somehow more dangerous than the sneer. "Because McNair wanted you alive. He needed you on that ship doing your job. We were under strict orders to stay out of your way."

"You call leaving us stranded staying out of my way?"

He shrugged. "You're alive, aren't you?"

Yeah, but she didn't know for how long.

"Javier, hurry up. McNair wants us back at the ship in fifteen. We have to get out to the site before the storm hits." One of the others hollered.

Javier, who still gripped her arm, yelled back, "I'm hurrying, Chris."

"The charges are loaded." One of the other guys threw back his head and laughed. "A couple hours and there'll be a huge kaboom."

Chris smacked the guy in the back of the head. "Shut it, idiot." He tossed a pointed look in her direction.

"Please. Like anyone will believe her if she says something. McNair just told the entire world that she's a fraud."

A sense of dread filled her belly. Because the guy was right.

KNOX'S CELL PHONE rang for the third time in three minutes. He really didn't feel like dealing with whatever Kennedy wanted to tell him, but realized if he didn't answer she was simply going to keep calling. Better to deal with it now.

Besides, drinking wasn't exactly working for him. He'd ordered a Scotch on the rocks fifteen minutes earlier and had barely taken a sip.

He'd welcomed the smooth fire as it had slipped down his throat and spread through his belly.

But he wanted Avery more.

Too bad he couldn't have her.

"What?" he growled.

"Turn on a TV. Now," was Kennedy's only response.

Reaching for the remote to the TV behind the bar, Knox flipped it on. "What am I supposed to be looking for?"

The words weren't out of his mouth two seconds before they became unnecessary. Scrolling to one of the major news channels, he saw Avery filling the screen.

A voice spoke over the picture for a few seconds. "This is the press conference Anderson McNair called several minutes ago," the anchor said.

"I told you I didn't want to see this," Knox growled into the phone, his thumb on the off button.

Before he could push Kennedy said, "Watch. Trust me."

He didn't remember hanging up, but he must have. His eyes were glued to the screen. Avery was beautiful, calm and perfectly in control on the surface.

Although, he saw beneath that. Noticed her lips part as if she was breathing quickly. The heavy way she swallowed. The fear and pain and guilt she couldn't quite banish from her eyes.

He didn't want it to matter, but it did.

Even more when he finally heard her say the wreck was the *Chimera*.

He was standing, the remote biting into his hand beneath the force of his grip as he watched a guy who was clearly hired muscle lead her off the stage. But what McNair said next sent a cascade of unpleasant emotions through his chest.

Avery hadn't earned her doctorate.

Knox shook his head, unsure how to even process that information. It wasn't good, if it was true. And, considering he'd known all along that Avery was hiding something, it made perfect sense.

What the hell happened now?

Not just with the *Chimera*, but with Avery?

She'd still betrayed him and Trident, even if it hadn't been the way he'd thought. She'd lied to them. To everyone.

But the Avery he knew wouldn't have done something like that without a good reason.

Knox's brain was still spinning when he heard a commotion at the entrance to the hotel bar.

"I need to see him immediately. It's urgent."

"I'm sorry, ma'am, it's hotel policy not to provide information about our guests. If you'd like to leave your contact information I'd be happy to provide Mr. McLemore with a message."

Knox reached into his wallet, pulled out a wad of cash without really looking to see what it was, and tossed it onto the bar. He was across the lobby of the hotel, grasping Avery's arms before he even registered the intent.

"Avery."

The relief that chased across her face was nearly his undoing, but he steeled his resolve.

"What's going on?"

"We have to go, right now."

She tried to tug at him, but he planted his feet and didn't budge. "I'm not going anywhere with you."

She made a small, wounded sound and recoiled from him. For a second he regretted his harsh words, but he couldn't quite banish the part of him that wanted to hurt her as she'd hurt him. It was selfish and petty, but there nonetheless.

"Look, I know you're pissed at me and have good reason, but McNair is going to do something to the *Chimera*."

"What are you talking about?"

A bark of frustration rumbled through her throat. "The drug runner who left us on that island, he was there today. With McNair. And I heard another couple of his guys talking about explosives."

"What?"

"They were friends, Knox. Business partners. McNair's diving company is a front for running drugs in the Caribbean. Think about it, this explains a lot."

Knox had to admit she was right. He'd thought all along that something about the drug runners and the situation with McNair was off, he just couldn't figure out what.

"And since I just ruined his attempt to interrupt the salvage of the *Chimera* by announcing the truth, he's planning on something else. Something big. Something with explosives."

She gripped his arms, pulling herself up onto her tiptoes. "Knox, we have to stop him. Please." Tears swam at the base of her lashes. "We can't let him get away with this. The *Chimera* is too important.

Grasping her hand, he said, "Let's go."

# 15

BEFORE THEY WERE out of the bar, Knox had his phone pressed to his ear. "Kennedy, find me the fastest boat you can. I need to get to the *Chimera* right away."

Avery listened as Knox relayed the details to Trident's office manager. Jumping into the rental car, they headed back to the marina without stopping for anything.

A few minutes later, Kennedy got back to them with information for a speedboat rental. She also let them know that the crew had been contacted and a select few—with military training—were meeting them.

The group meeting them had grabbed some supplies from the *Amphitrite*. Avery didn't want to think about what was inside the bags as they were loaded on to the rental boat, but she couldn't help it. The bags had to be full of weapons. What else would they bring?

The men moved together like a well-oiled machine, Knox right at the forefront directing everyone.

Within minutes of arriving they were bobbing against the increasingly choppy water. The boat was fast, but was it fast enough?

Dread twisted through Avery's belly.

Knox had tried to leave her at the dock, but she'd cut

the argument short by climbing on board. He could have carried her off again, but they both knew they didn't have time to waste.

He'd glared at her, but left her alone.

Knox had made call after call from the moment they'd entered the boat.

Avery sat at the back, alone. Everyone else, the men who'd been friendly with her just hours ago, acted as if she wasn't even there.

But she couldn't dredge up the energy to care. What they thought of her didn't matter nearly as much as protecting the *Chimera*.

The clouds overhead swirled angrily. Wind buffeted from all sides. It didn't take long for rain to start lashing against them. She wasn't sure if it was from the storm or the speed at which they were flying across the roiling surface, but the drops pelted her, stinging.

She huddled down, trying to make herself as small as possible.

God, were they going to make it in time?

Closing her eyes, Avery sent up a prayer. A warm arm settled around her shoulders, pulling her tight into the shelter of a large body.

She didn't need to open her eyes to know it was Knox. She recognized the feel of him. The scent of him, even rain drenched.

Avery buried her face in his chest, accepting the comfort for however long he was willing to give it to her.

"He used the information about your PhD as blackmail," Knox murmured in her ear.

It wasn't a question, but she nodded her head. "It was after Melody OD'd. When she'd been arrested for possession several years before, my parents had disowned her. Even when she OD'd, they refused to help her. But I couldn't just abandon her. I left school, but had already accepted a position on an upcoming project. They never asked for proof of my graduation so I just...didn't give it to them. I always intended to go back, but..."

"That was the find that made your career," Knox finished softly.

She'd been part of the team to discover evidence of an ancient city off the coast of the Mediterranean. She'd found herself interviewed by major archaeological publications, the subject-matter expert consulted on multiple documentaries.

"I needed the money for Melody's care. I couldn't pass up the opportunities that discovery opened for me."

He nodded. Avery tipped her head up, not caring about the rain that fell onto her face because she wanted to see him. He watched her, his expression shuttered.

Was this him getting closure?

And if that was all he wanted from her, didn't she owe it to him?

"McNair threatened her. She's helpless, with the mind of a child. She can barely tie her own shoes, Knox, and the asshole threatened her when I started arguing that I couldn't give him what he wanted."

She was still afraid he'd find some way to follow through on the threat. The damage had already been done to her career, but there were still plenty of ways McNair could hurt her, including harming Melody.

"She'll be fine, Avery. I promise."

Pulling his cell from his pocket, Knox made a quick call. She had no idea who he was talking to, but from his end of the conversation it was clear he was arranging for someone to keep an eye on her sister.

Tears mixed with rain, flowing over her eyelashes and down her cheeks.

It had been a hell of a long time since anyone had been there to help with her problems. Until Knox shouldered some of the weight—without being asked—she hadn't realized how heavy the responsibilities had become.

She wouldn't trade them for anything. Melody was her sister, end of discussion. And no matter her mistakes, she was paying for them, the price higher than anyone could expect.

"Thank you," she whispered, trying to get hold of her emotions again.

"Why didn't you tell me, Avery? I could have helped."

She just shook her head. "I've been alone for so long. And I was comfortable that way. It's hard to place my faith in anyone. You were different, though. It wasn't that I didn't want to let you in, I just didn't know how."

His palm cupped her cheek, warm and wide. With his thumb, he tipped her head back so she was staring up into his eyes.

And what she saw there made her breath catch. Softness, pain, hope...love.

"After the accident that killed my brother—the accident that was my fault—I didn't care about anything, including my own life. I can't tell you how many times I wished I'd died that night with him. I thought it would have been easier."

Avery sucked in a harsh breath. Hearing Knox, one of the strongest men she'd ever met, admit to that kind of despair felt so wrong. She wanted to wrap her trembling arms around him and hold him tight.

His fingers tangled in her wet hair, flexing and pulling her closer.

"I was wrong. Jackson and Asher helped me realize that to a certain extent. Their friendship saved me, more than they probably realize. Before them, I was alone. By choice. But life isn't meant to be lived that way, Avery.

"The Teams showed me a brotherhood that goes so deep it's more than a bond forged in fear and blood. It's a turn of phrase people like to throw around—I'd die for him, kill for her—but for us it's real and everyday."

His thumbs slipped across her cheeks, down her jawline, over her lips.

"That kind of connection is important, but with you… there's more. You're important to me, Avery. I need you in my life. And I'd do anything for you."

The tears were back, because she wanted what he was offering her, but she didn't deserve it. "I lied to you."

"Yeah, I figured that out."

"I'm so sorry." A heavy lump settled in her throat. Avery needed his forgiveness or there was no way they could move forward. Her entire body vibrated with the certainty that he wouldn't be able to look at her the same way ever again, not when her life, the woman he'd thought she was, was built on a lie.

"I don't care, Avery. So you don't have a damn piece of paper. You're good at your job. You know what you're talking about, and that experience is a hell of a lot more important."

"But…"

"Look, if anyone understands how one decision can screw an entire life, it's me. I'm not the kind of man to judge a person by their mistakes, but by what they do about them."

She stared up at him for several moments, overwhelmed. Once again, he'd demonstrated to her the kind of man he was, honorable and understanding.

"God, you make it so easy to love you."

Knox laughed, the sound rushing out of him with surprise. "I do, huh? Pretty sure you're the only person who's ever thought so."

Avery smiled, something she definitely hadn't expected to be doing when the day started. "Absolutely, and I should know. But, please, don't do something stupid when I've only just found you. Knox, you can't go after McNair alone."

"I'm not. I've already called a contact with the Coast Guard and they've notified their counterparts. A joint task force is meeting us at the dive site."

Relief had Avery sagging against him.

"Hey, hey." Pulling her up into his arms, Knox settled her in his lap. He found her lips, sinking them both into the heat of the kiss.

And she let him distract her, because she had no idea what they would find when they reached the *Chimera*, or if they would make it out alive considering they were barreling straight into a hurricane.

BEN THROTTLED DOWN the boat. Speed had been important, but now they needed stealth. Before heading out, they'd grabbed the guns and ammo Trident kept stocked on the *Amphitrite*.

Knox had been hoping not to need it, but it was obvious they'd arrived before the authorities, and he couldn't afford to wait and give McNair the opportunity to get charges in the water.

Nodding to the handful of men he'd brought with him, they began preparing.

"I thought you said you'd called the police or whatever." Avery said, her voice going shrill.

Grasping her by the shoulders, Knox turned her away from the flurry of activity and to him. "I did, but they aren't here yet and we can't wait."

The storm had increased, wind whipping so hard it practically tore the words out of his mouth.

"The hurricane is getting closer. These are just feeder bands right now and they're bad enough, but when the real storm hits in a few hours…" They'd already heard reports of waterspouts.

He should have fought harder to make Avery stay onshore. His stomach clenched into a hard fist. If anything happened to her, he'd never forgive himself. He already lived with so much regret, he couldn't handle adding more.

"I need you to promise me you'll stay on the boat, Avery."

She shook her head. "I'm coming with you."

"You'll be a distraction. I can't do my job if I'm worried about protecting you."

"This isn't your job anymore, Knox."

"It is today."

Her eyes, big and blue, pulled down in the corners with fear and sadness.

"I have the skills and training, doc." He smoothed away the strands of hair sticking to her wet cheeks. "I'll be fine. As long as I know you're here safe. Please, give me this."

Reluctantly, she nodded.

He heard a shout from the front of the boat. McNair's ship came into view and it was past time for talking.

Knox instructed Ben to bring them alongside McNair's boat where it had been anchored. His guys grabbed on, boosting themselves up and over onto McNair's deck. The men Knox had brought on this mission were up for the task—two Navy sailors, an ex-Marine and an ex-Ranger. Avery had told them McNair had six men at the press conference, but it was possible he'd picked up more.

Still, Knox liked his odds. These guys were good.

They stayed low as they crept across the deck, expecting shots to ring out at any moment, but everything was quiet. Too quiet.

Knox waited until he was certain Ben had headed off, taking Avery a safe distance away, before turning his focus to the mission at hand.

It was late afternoon, but the angry storm clouds made it dark and gray.

He wished he had comm equipment. Trident would be investing as soon as they got out of this mess. Even if they never had to use it, it would be worth having.

He used hand signals to send his guys sweeping through the ship. Clearing the deck, they headed below, subduing two men who were too busy drinking beer to notice they'd been boarded in the first place.

Knox fought the sensation that he was a step behind. He'd felt out of sync this entire time, knowing there was more going on with McNair, but unable to figure out what it was.

"None of this makes any goddamn sense," he growled out once everyone was gathered back on deck.

"There are no launches aboard."

He'd noticed that as well, but he'd swept the area, looking for evidence that they were already diving, placing the explosives. Knox was familiar enough with the coordinates of the wreckage to know they weren't.

Maybe they'd been tipped off and rather than fight had left on the launches. Avery had mentioned she thought someone else on the Trident team was compromised. How else would McNair have known about their relationship?

He'd deal with that later.

The cell in his pocket vibrated. Pulling it out, he recognized Avery's number.

"I'm fine, doc," he said.

"That's nice," said a gruff voice. "But Ms. Walsh isn't.

Perhaps you'd like to return to your boat and rescue her. You do have a bit of a hero complex, Knox."

His hands fisted helplessly by his side. "What do you want, McNair?"

An engine rumbled in the distance, getting louder and louder. It was too much to hope that it was the authorities finally arriving.

Dread settled like a stone as he watched the speedboat they'd rented approach the ship again.

Four figures gathered together. Ben was at the wheel, steering them back. Next to him stood another man, his knees bent as his body moved with the fluid motion of the boat. Behind them, McNair stood, his back lodged against the side of the boat with his arm wrapped hard around Avery's throat, holding her up on her toes and cutting off her air.

Ben throttled back the engine and they drifted close. Knox's finger twitched on the trigger of his gun, trained on the man holding his woman.

"I wouldn't try that, Knox. You might hit Avery, and I'd hate for you to have to watch someone else you love die right in front of your eyes."

Knox sucked in a harsh breath. Avery whimpered, although he didn't think it was because McNair had caused her physical pain.

She stared at him, her eyes wide. They weren't filled with fear as he'd expected, but resolve.

"Don't," he whispered, hoping McNair would think he was talking to him instead of Avery. "Please, don't do anything stupid."

Helplessness filled him, a heavy weight that was hard to bear. He'd experienced it before and had hoped never to feel the sensation again.

"Drop your weapons, gentlemen."

The men behind him hesitated until he nodded. McNair was right. He was a damn good shot, but couldn't risk hitting Avery instead of the asshole holding her like a shield.

"Now, there's a simple way for us all to get what we want."

"And what's that, McNair? What do you want?"

A feral smile twisted the other man's lips. Knox's eyes flicked to the man beside Ben, not surprised to realize, now that they were closer, it was the drug runner they'd encountered before. What he didn't see was a gun trained on his captain. And the fact that Ben refused to look him in the eye made his stomach clench with anger and dread.

"First, I want you to call whoever is headed this way and tell them you were misinformed, that there's no one at the site."

Knox hesitated, trying to figure out a way to give McNair what he wanted without calling off their one chance at tipping the scales in their favor.

McNair slammed the butt of his gun into the side of Avery's head. She slumped in his hold and he let her go, not even bothering to cushion her fall as she collapsed into the bottom of the boat.

"Quickly, Knox, or I'll be forced to do something worse. I know you've been shot before, but I'd wager your beautiful girlfriend hasn't had the misfortune to experience that kind of pain…yet."

He wanted to hurt the man and if they hadn't been separated by several feet of roiling sea he would have. But letting his anger rule him right now would only put Avery in further jeopardy. Knox glared at McNair as he pulled his cell from his pocket.

"On speaker, if you don't mind," McNair hollered in a pleasant voice that scraped along Knox's last nerve.

He watched a trickle of blood, mixed with the rain

pouring over them, roll down Avery's temple even as he placed the call.

"I'm going to find you, McNair, and make you pay for every drop of her blood that you've spilled."

"I'm certain you'll try."

The call connected, crackling across the airspace. "McLemore, we're fifteen minutes out."

"Don't bother. We were wrong, he isn't here."

The voice on the other end was silent for a moment as static rolled out. "We're almost there. We can consult when we arrive."

"No," Knox said, his voice going hard. "The storm is getting worse. We don't have fifteen minutes to wait. We can meet back in Nassau."

"All right."

The line went dead. "Satisfied?" he asked, throwing a daggered stare at McNair.

"Not hardly."

That was good, because neither was Knox. He needed to get onto that boat, but how to make it happen?

He was running through options, discarding everything because each plan involved a few seconds that left Avery open and vulnerable—a risk he wouldn't take—when he saw her stir. It was a minuscule twitch.

Dread wrenched him. He knew Avery was about to do something insanely brave and dangerous and he couldn't stop her. Or hold in his howl of frustration. McNair chuckled, momentarily distracted, and didn't see Avery's leg sweeping toward him until it was too late.

From ten feet away, Knox was unable to do anything but watch. McNair yelped, his body pitching backward. He landed with a thud. Avery was on top of him, gripping his wrist in her hand, banging it and the gun he held repeatedly against the hard edge of the bench beside them.

She had skill, but McNair had experience and about a hundred pounds on her.

Without even thinking about it, Knox vaulted over the railing and plunged into the churning water. He sank for a few seconds before kicking up, searching for breath. Powerful waves crashed down over his head.

Knox heard the crack of a gun firing, the echo ricocheting across the water.

Two more followed in quick succession.

"No!" he roared. If Avery died he was going to lose it.

Breaking out in a hard stroke, he closed the gap to the boat. Gripping the side, he hauled himself up and over, bracing for a gruesome sight. His mind was already predicting Avery's blood spilling out across the deck.

And there was blood, but it wasn't hers.

Avery stood there, drenched and bedraggled. Her bright red hair hung in wet strands down her back and stuck to her damp cheeks.

She was trembling, her entire body moving with the force of the shivers wracking her.

Her eyes were trained down at the man stretched out at her feet, two gaping bullet holes in his chest.

Knox didn't stop moving until he'd wrapped her in his arms, propelling them both to the far side of the boat.

He was aware enough to realize the drug runner had also crumpled to the bottom of the boat, a wound in his shoulder oozing blood. He wasn't dead, but he wasn't an immediate threat. Ben slumped to the deck, the back of his head seeping blood where he'd cracked it against the side of the boat.

"I killed him," Avery whispered, her voice low and ragged.

Knox cupped her cheeks with his hands. Her skin was

ice-cold. Forcing her to look away from McNair's body, he turned her face to his.

"Baby. It's okay. You're okay." He ran his hands over her body, making sure the words he'd just spoken were true. Aside from the cut at her temple, she seemed unharmed.

"I killed him, Knox." Her mouth moved slowly, as if it had frozen and she was forcing her lips to move.

"I know. But he was going to hurt you. You did the right thing."

She blinked and then blinked again before nodding. Slowly, color returned to her face. She made a sound, a smothered whimper, and buried her face in his chest.

"I was so scared," she mumbled into him.

Knox wrapped his arms tightly around her, taking her weight.

"Ben drove the boat straight to McNair. He's the Trident leak."

Disbelief and rage rolled through Knox. Ben had been with them almost from the beginning. But he'd deal with their captain later. Right now, Avery was his main concern.

"God, Avery. If anything had happened to you…" Pulling her away, Knox looked at her again, just to make sure she really was standing there and unharmed. "I don't think I could have survived losing you, Avery. I love you."

Her stiff lips curved into a sad smile. "I love you too."

She clung to him. Together, they collapsed onto a seat at the back of the boat, as far away from the carnage as they could. Around them, chaos reigned. Bahamian government officials, accompanied by the US Coast Guard screamed onto the scene. Apparently, they'd heard the gunshots.

The storm raged, picking up strength, lashing them with wind and rain that had their boat rocking wickedly.

But none of that mattered, because Avery was wrapped tight in his arms. Safe and sound. His.

Nothing was going to convince him to let her go.

# *Epilogue*

AVERY STARED OUT across the crystal-clear blue sea. As long as she lived, the view would never get old.

She felt Knox's strong arms circle her waist from behind.

"What are you doing out here, Dr. Walsh?"

While her business had definitely taken a hit thanks to McNair's announcement about her lack of a PhD, it turned out things hadn't been quite as bad as she'd feared. It helped that McNair himself had been exposed as a fraud and high-level drug dealer. Although, that information didn't change the truth about her own duplicity.

Yes, she'd lost clients, but she deserved that. What had surprised her was the number of people who felt the same way Knox did—that she was an expert with or without the degree.

But completing her PhD had become something she needed to do for herself. So as soon as she could, Avery had contacted Texas International University to begin the process of finishing her program. And would hopefully have everything squared away in the next few months. Making that call had been difficult, but Knox had been right beside her.

Just as she'd been by his side as they'd dealt with the fallout from McNair and the hurricane.

In the aftermath it had become clear that McNair was a major player in the Caribbean drug market.

The task force had taken his wounded accomplice into custody, a man they'd been trying to capture for several years. With the evidence found on McNair's ship, they'd also arrested most of his crew.

Ben had been spared arrest but lost his position with Trident. McNair had been blackmailing him as well. What had saved him in the end was the fact that when Avery went after McNair, Ben had tried to take down the drug runner, getting injured in the process. But that had given Avery enough time to get a shot off and at least incapacitate McNair.

What had made Avery sick was the quantity of sophisticated explosives they'd found on board McNair's launch, no doubt intended for the *Chimera*. They'd come so close to losing everything.

Luckily, everyone had made it back to land in time to seek shelter from the hurricane, which had changed course, moving out to open sea.

The storm had skirted the *Chimera*'s location so she hadn't taken a direct hit. They'd still had to spend several weeks surveying the wreck just to be safe, but she'd come through without any damage.

Although the close call made the entire Trident team eager to move forward with the salvage as quickly as safety would allow.

Now, six weeks later, the wreck was stabilized and they were ready to see what secrets she held.

The excitement was palpable.

Avery was just grateful the Trident team was allowing her to stay on the project.

"You ready for this, doc?" Knox whispered against her ear.

Leaning back into his arms, Avery realized that with him she could tackle anything.

Together they'd gone to visit Melody. She'd loved introducing him to her sister. They'd hit it off immediately. Melody smiled softly every time Knox came into the room.

But it had made Avery's heart ache when, in a rare moment they were alone, Melody had looked at her with a serious expression and said, "He cares a lot for you. You're so lucky."

She mourned that her sister would never experience what she had with Knox. But she'd learned to let the past—and the things that might have been—go. Melody was happy and that was what mattered most.

Knox had convinced Avery to move in with him just that morning. Although she should probably have been pissed at his methods, considering he'd had her mindless beneath him at the time.

She couldn't be upset, though, since it was what she wanted too. He'd even found a facility in Florida that they could move Melody to once her doctors decided she could handle the transition. One with even better programs that might improve Melody's quality of life even more.

Avery and Knox had both been through hell in their lives, lost people, lost pieces of themselves. He had helped her open up, realize she didn't have to be afraid of letting people in. Over the past few weeks, the circle of people in her life had widened.

And she was grateful. Surprisingly, she was enjoying getting to know Jackson, Loralei and Kennedy better. Asher had welcomed her to the group with a huge hug and smacking kiss on the cheek that had Knox growling a warning. They'd accepted her immediately as one of their own, despite knowing what she'd done.

Luckily, in light of McNair's activities and her discovery of the medal, the US court had ruled in Trident's favor, awarding them exclusive salvage rights.

That sense of camaraderie—family—was something she hadn't had in a while. Knox had given that back to her.

In return, he'd opened up about his brother, the accident, the life he'd led with the Teams. Each day Knox proved over and over that he was a man she was lucky to have in her life.

She tipped her head back, and Knox sealed his mouth to hers. The world tilted, and as always, she sank into the delicious kiss. By the time he let her up, Avery had forgotten where they were and what they'd been doing. All she could see, hear and feel was him.

Knox grinned down at her, mischief brightening his gaze.

Avery loved him best like this—open, honest, giving, playful. She needed that, more than she'd ever realized.

"Let's go find some gold, doc."

\* \* \* \* \*

*Asher Reynolds is determined to steer clear of his friend's little sister. But it's not so easy when they're trapped together on a ship. And sweet little Kennedy may not be as innocent as she seems...*

*Look for UNDER PRESSURE (November 2015), the final installment of Kira Sinclair's SEALS OF FORTUNE miniseries.*

COMING NEXT MONTH FROM

## Available August 4, 2015

### #855 ROLLING LIKE THUNDER
*Thunder Mountain Brotherhood*
by Vicki Lewis Thompson

Chelsea Trask might just be able to save the financially troubled ranch Finn O'Roarke once called home—if the scorching chemistry between her and the sexy brewmaster leaves them any time to work at all!

### #856 THE MIGHTY QUINNS: DEVIN
*The Mighty Quinns*
by Kate Hoffmann

When Elodie Winchester returns to her hometown, Sheriff Devin Cassidy wants to reignite the passion between them, even if it costs him everything he's worked for...and exposes a shocking family secret.

### #857 SEX, LIES AND DESIGNER SHOES
by Kimberly Van Meter

Rian Dalton likes to keep his business separate from pleasure. Until he meets client CoCo Abelli, an heiress with a reckless streak. Now Rian can't keep his hands to himself!

### #858 A COWBOY RETURNS
*Wild Western Heat*
by Kelli Ireland

*He's back.* Eli Covington was Regan Matthews's first love—but not the man she married. Working together to save his New Mexico ranch brings up old feelings that are far too tempting to resist.

---

# REQUEST YOUR FREE BOOKS!
## 2 FREE NOVELS PLUS 2 FREE GIFTS!

### HARLEQUIN®

*Blaze*

### red-hot reads!

**YES!** Please send me 2 FREE Harlequin® Blaze® novels and my 2 FREE gifts (gifts are worth about $10). After receiving them, if I don't wish to receive any more books, I can return the shipping statement marked "cancel." If I don't cancel, I will receive 4 brand-new novels every month and be billed just $4.74 per book in the U.S. or $5.21 per book in Canada. That's a savings of at least 14% off the cover price. It's quite a bargain. Shipping and handling is just 50¢ per book in the U.S. and 75¢ per book in Canada.* I understand that accepting the 2 free books and gifts places me under no obligation to buy anything. I can always return a shipment and cancel at any time. Even if I never buy another book, the two free books and gifts are mine to keep forever.

150/350 HDN GH2D

Name _____ (PLEASE PRINT) _____

Address _____ Apt. # _____

City _____ State/Prov. _____ Zip/Postal Code _____

Signature (if under 18, a parent or guardian must sign) _____

### Mail to the **Reader Service:**
**IN U.S.A.:** P.O. Box 1867, Buffalo, NY 14240-1867
**IN CANADA:** P.O. Box 609, Fort Erie, Ontario L2A 5X3

**Want to try two free books from another line?**
**Call 1-800-873-8635 or visit www.ReaderService.com.**

\* Terms and prices subject to change without notice. Prices do not include applicable taxes. Sales tax applicable in N.Y. Canadian residents will be charged applicable taxes. Offer not valid in Quebec. This offer is limited to one order per household. Not valid for current subscribers to Harlequin Blaze books. All orders subject to credit approval. Credit or debit balances in a customer's account(s) may be offset by any other outstanding balance owed by or to the customer. Please allow 4 to 6 weeks for delivery. Offer available while quantities last.

**Your Privacy**—The Reader Service is committed to protecting your privacy. Our Privacy Policy is available online at www.ReaderService.com or upon request from the Reader Service.

We make a portion of our mailing list available to reputable third parties that offer products we believe may interest you. If you prefer that we not exchange your name with third parties, or if you wish to clarify or modify your communication preferences, please visit us at www.ReaderService.com/consumerchoice or write to us at Reader Service Preference Service, P.O. Box 9062, Buffalo, NY 14240-9062. Include your complete name and address.

HB15

SPECIAL EXCERPT FROM

**H** HARLEQUIN®

*Blaze*

*Police Chief Devin Cassidy can't resist reigniting the
passion between him and Elodie Winchester, even
if it costs him everything—and exposes a shocking
connection to the Quinn family.*

*Here's a sneak preview of*
**THE MIGHTY QUINNS: DEVIN**,
*the latest steamy installment in*
**Kate Hoffmann**'s
*beloved miniseries*
**THE MIGHTY QUINNS**.

Elodie hurried downstairs and threw open the front door.
She stepped out into the storm, running across the lawn.
When she reached the police cruiser, she stopped. "What
are you doing out here?" she shouted above the wind.

Dev slowly got out of the car, his hand braced along the
top of the door. "I couldn't sleep."

"I couldn't, either," she shouted.

It was all he needed. He stepped toward her and before
she knew it, she was in his arms, his hands smoothing over
the rain-soaked fabric of her dress. His lips covered hers in
a desperate, deeply powerful kiss. He molded her mouth to
his, still searching for something even more intimate.

The fabric of her dress clung to her naked skin, a feeble
barrier to his touch. Elodie fought the urge to reach for the
hem of her dress and pull it over her head. They were on a
public street, with houses all around.

"Come with me," she murmured. She laced her fingers through his and pulled him toward the house.

Once they reached the protection of the veranda, he grabbed her waist again, pulling her into another kiss. Dev smoothed his hand up her torso until he found her breast and he cupped it, his thumb teasing at her taut nipple.

Elodie reached for the hem of his shirt, but it was tucked underneath his leather utility belt. "Take this off," she murmured, frantically searching for the buckle.

He carefully unclipped his gun and set it on a nearby table. A moment later, his utility belt dropped to the ground, followed by his badge and, finally, his shirt. Her palms skimmed over hard muscle and smooth skin. His shoulders, once slight, were now broad, his torso a perfect V.

Dev reached for the hem of her dress and bunched it in his fists, pulling it higher and higher until it was twisted around her waist. He gently pushed her back against the door and she moaned as his fingertips skimmed the soft skin of her inner thigh.

Wild sensations raced through her body and she trembled as she anticipated what would come next…

*Don't miss*
*THE MIGHTY QUINNS: DEVIN by Kate Hoffmann,*
*available August 2015 wherever*
*Harlequin® Blaze® books and ebooks are sold.*

www.Harlequin.com

HBEXP0715

# Love the Harlequin book you just read?

Your opinion matters.

Review this book on your favorite book site, review site, blog or your own social media properties and share your opinion with other readers!

HARLEQUIN®

A *Romance* FOR EVERY MOOD™

# JUST CAN'T GET ENOUGH?

Join our social communities
and talk to us online.

You will have access to the latest
news on upcoming titles and special
promotions, but most importantly,
you can talk to other fans about your
favorite Harlequin reads.

Harlequin.com/Community

HSOCIAL

# HARLEQUIN®

A *Romance* FOR EVERY MOOD™

Stay up-to-date on all your
romance-reading news with the
*Harlequin Shopping Guide,*
featuring bestselling authors, exciting new
miniseries, books to watch and more!

The newest issue will be delivered right to you
with our compliments! There are 4 each year.

Signing up is easy.

## EMAIL

ShoppingGuide@Harlequin.ca

## WRITE TO US

HARLEQUIN BOOKS
Attention: Customer Service Department
P.O. Box 9057, Buffalo, NY 14269-9057

## OR PHONE

1-800-873-8635 in the United States
1-888-343-9777 in Canada

Please allow 4-6 weeks for delivery of the first issue by mail.

# THE WORLD IS BETTER WITH

## Romance

Harlequin has everything from contemporary, passionate and heartwarming to suspenseful and inspirational stories.

Whatever your mood,
we have a romance just for you!

Connect with us to find your next great read,
special offers and more.

 /HarlequinBooks

@HarlequinBooks

www.HarlequinBlog.com

www.Harlequin.com/Newsletters

A Romance FOR EVERY MOOD™

www.Harlequin.com

SERIESHALOAD2015